Praise

The Reincarnations: Stories

"Nathan Elias writes about the world—both as we know it and as we hadn't yet thought to imagine it—through a singular, deeply compassionate, lens, showing us both its monstrousness and its beauty. The stories in this collection are steeped in loss and grief, but they're also suffused with hope, with love, with the possibilities of transformation, of flight. After finishing *The Reincarnations*, I felt transformed, myself."

— **Gayle Brandeis,**
author of *Many Restless Concerns*

"Whether rendering the nuances of the Midwest or capturing the lush sensory details of Florida, Nathan Elias paints the heart of a place and the people who live there with a pointillist's accuracy. *The Reincarnations* portrays the complexities of interpersonal relationships and how these emotional kinships often lead to our unravelings. Through hotel rooms and over flaming mattresses, past alligator daughters and mermaid dolls and snake biologists and unusual pharmaceuticals, Elias shows us both the commonalities and rarities of what it means to be human."

— **JD Scott,**
author of *Moonflower, Nightshade,*
All the Hours of the Day

the

REINCARNATIONS

stories

Nathan Elias

MONTAG

First Montag Press E-Book and Paperback Original Edition September 2020

Copyright © 2020 by Nathan Elias

As the writer and creator of this story, Nathan Elias asserts the right to be identified as the author of this book.

Montag Press ISBN: 978-1-940233-83-3
Design © 2020 Amit Dey

Montag Press Team:
Photographer: A. Milano
Cover artist: Peter Selgin
Editor: Brandon Nolta
Managing Director: Charlie Franco

A Montag Press Book
www.montagpress.com
Montag Press
777 Morton Street, Unit B
San Francisco CA 94129 USA

Montag Press, the burning book with the hatchet cover, the skewed word mark and the portrayal of the long-suffering fireman mascot are trademarks of Montag Press.

Printed & Digitally Originated in the United States of America
10 9 8 7 6 5 4 3 2 1

For Alexi, with all my heart.

Time forks perpetually toward
innumerable futures.

—Jorge Luis Borges

Life rises out of death, death rises out of life;
in being opposite they yearn to each other,
they give birth to each other and are
forever reborn.

—Ursula K. Le Guin

Contents

THE REINCARNATIONS

The Alligator Theory

*C*ayman hadn't slept for five days, and he had begun to worry that he was losing touch with reality. While Alma knocked herself out with tequila just to get through another answerless night, Cayman plugged his video camera into a television in the garage and sat out there on the musty sofa they'd bought through OfferUp from an old Hispanic couple in Seminole Heights. He watched, over and over again, the footage he'd shot of his little girl since she was born. He kept the garage door open—he didn't care if the neighbors saw him in there, drunk and sobbing—in case, by some will of God, his sweetheart came home in the middle of the night.

This ritual began on the second night after she disappeared; he'd start with the first SD card—there were seventeen in total—dated October 31, 2014, the day his child had entered this ugly and terrifying world, and he'd watch all the footage leading up to October 31, 2018, the morning she was last seen. The fact that his little one had disappeared on her birthday only made the mystery more baffling, perhaps even that much more debilitating for Cayman and Alma, if such a thing were even possible.

Cayman kept a calendar hanging near the television. It was Monday, November 5, and their daughter had been gone for six whole days. For the first four days, Cayman and Alma were told to stay in a hotel outside the city while the police investigated their house. After that, the police performed a thorough sweep of Moss Park, including hounds and a dredge, but found nothing.

The sixth night, Cayman thought while he drank the remains of Alma's Cuervo, was the bringer of complete numbness. He felt the last of his sobs alleviating. He'd already faced madness, suicidal thoughts, and blinding rage. Now, with the onset of rain and a breeze coming in through the garage door, Cayman hoped he could finally try to instill some logic into the totally illogical tragedy that had befallen him and his wife. As the wind picked up, he heard rustling in the oak, cypress, and palm trees outside. The quiet whistle was soft, sweet as a child's voice. Cayman stood from the couch and went to the garage door, its dark outline like a monster's gaping mouth. If the garage door is a monster's mouth, he thought, then the rest of the world is its body, and my little girl has been swallowed whole. Raindrops splashed on his bare feet and, for a moment, he thought he heard someone saying "Daddy."

He ran out into the rain and called his daughter's name. The wind picked up around him, its whistle louder than before.

"Tina!" he called. "Tina! Where are you, baby?"

He went down the driveway and into the street where a small stream of oily water reflected the moonlight and sped into the gutter. It made him think of how God might have looked down upon the Hillsborough River, where he, Alma, and Tina had picnicked only moments before Tina vanished.

He screamed her name again and saw one of the neighbors' lights turn on across the street. Stupid, he thought. She isn't here. She isn't anywhere.

"Stupid," he said and slapped himself, again and again. "Stupid, stupid, stupid!" It didn't matter if the neighbors saw him beating himself up. He wanted the world, the ugly monster, to see how much he hated himself. Once his face felt good and raw, he went back inside and sat, soaked, on the already dank couch. The television was blue, which meant that it was time for another SD card. He inserted the next one, pushed play on the camera, and let out an extinguishing sigh of relief when he saw Tina's face pop up on the screen.

"Wake up, Cay."

When he opened his eyes, he saw Alma standing over him in her pink, ragged robe. He smelled the remnants of a hard Florida downpour—humidity, grass, and oil hanging thick in the air. A breeze came in through the garage door. It had been his first sleep since Tina disappeared, and it felt as refreshing as it was disorienting.

"You're going to catch cold if you keep leaving that damned door open," Alma said. She picked up her empty bottle of Cuervo from next to the television and groaned.

"I need it open," he said, "in case she comes back in the middle of the night."

"If she comes back, it won't be through that door."

"Not *if*," Cayman said. "She's coming back."

Alma turned the television off, tossed the Cuervo bottle into the recycling bin, and went back into the house.

Before Tina, Cayman had devoted his career to making documentaries about anomalies. He'd long been fascinated with things in life that couldn't quite be explained. The known miracles in the world, the beautiful and profound things that people took for granted, lit a fire in him that made him want to document it, capture it to focus the world's attention on that which it overlooked. The metamorphosis of butterflies, for example, had intrigued him since he was a child. Two years before the baby, when he and Alma had only been together for six months, he invited her on a road trip to Coconut Creek where he'd been given a grant to film metamorphoses at Butterfly World.

"But don't they already have that on YouTube?" Alma had asked on the drive from Tennessee to Florida. "Haven't hundreds of people already filmed caterpillars turning into butterflies?"

All Cayman could do was shake his head. He tried to explain his zest for capturing things through his own lens, that it was more about the first-hand experience than adding to the canon of pre-existing footage. There was something breathtaking about rolling the camera, he'd said, and capturing the simple magic of nature.

"I want you to experience it with me," he told her. "I want you to be next to me, filming chrysalises. Who cares about YouTube? To see a butterfly emerge from its chrysalis in real life, without a screen, is something everyone should see at least once in their lifetime." Even though they'd only been together less than a year, he knew that he wanted to marry her. Proposing during metamorphosis, he believed, was probably the most romantic thing he'd ever come up with on his own.

Alma laughed. "I like the way you say *chrysalis*."

"Besides, the grant isn't just for caterpillars and butter-flies," Cayman said. "I pitched a documentary series about the wonders of metamorphosis. The caterpillar-to-butterfly transformation is only the first and most obvious in a series of transformations. Tadpoles and frogs are another great example. Dragonflies, too. They go through nymph stages instead of the chrysalis stage."

"There you go again," Alma said. She'd leaned across the armrest between them and put her lips to his ear. "Chrysalis. *Chrys-a-lis.*"

❧

They'd moved to Florida when Cayman was offered the position as producer at Bay News. Although his documentaries hadn't brought him the acclaim or notoriety he'd hoped for, the producer gig paid enough that he and Alma could finally make a home for themselves, have a family. He'd met her in his first week out of Los Angeles—they were both on the cusp of thirty—and he would have been happy settling down with her in Tennessee. But she wanted to start a family away from her home. "Somewhere new," she'd said, "but still in the South." They'd tried to get pregnant for months, and Cayman had started to worry that one of them was incapable. He'd known no greater joy than when Alma told him the test was positive. Another form of metamorphosis, Cayman thought. A woman transitioning into motherhood, a man into fatherhood. Alma agreed, hesitantly, to allow Cayman to document their life throughout the pregnancy.

❧

Every time Cayman went over the events leading up to Tina's disappearance, they made less and less sense. The three of them had gone to Moss Park for Tina's birthday picnic. Later, they were expecting friends and relatives to come over for a party. The picnic, however, was just for the three of them. Moss Park was small, barely a mile from their house. It faced the Hillsborough River and was canopied with trees covered in Spanish moss. "You know, Spanish moss isn't even from Spain," Alma had told them when they moved to Florida. "It's actually native to Mexico. And it's technically not moss, either. It's a bromeliad, which means that it's in the same family as pineapple." Cayman thought of this every time they went to Moss Park, every time he saw one of those trees that seemed to be melting like the clocks in the Dali paintings. For the birthday picnic, they'd brought a checkered blanket, a wicker basket, and peanut butter and banana sandwiches—Tina's favorite. They ate their sandwiches, played a quick game of tag, and lay down on the blanket. The last thing Cayman remembered was staring up at the sky through a patch of moss and pointing at a cloud.

"What do you see?" he'd asked his daughter. "I see a dinosaur."

"I see a bunny rabbit," Alma said.

"I see a cloud!" Tina said and giggled. "A big fluffy one."

Cayman and Alma laughed, and before Cayman knew it, he'd dozed off in the warm sunlight.

Upon opening his eyes, he immediately realized that Tina was no longer between him and Alma.

"Tina?" He shot up and shook Alma, who'd also been napping. "Alma, where's Tina?"

Cayman stood and looked around the park. There was nobody else there but them, nor had there been since they'd arrived. Cayman screamed Tina's name again and yanked Alma, a bit fiercely, onto her feet. "Look over there behind those trees," he ordered. "I'm going to check by the water."

He ran toward the river, heart pounding, and scanned the shrubs along the bank. He stepped into a thicket and saw a shrub rustling.

"Tina," he said and reached forward. His hand grazed something cold and muscular. He couldn't grab hold of it; it slipped through his fingers. He lunged forward and saw something submerge into the water. Something long and gray. Small rivets protruded from the surface of the water.

An alligator.

"Oh god," Cayman said. He jumped into the river and dove toward the rivets.

He couldn't feel anything, so he opened his eyes underwater, though he saw nothing but murky clouds of mud. He stayed under until he thought his lungs would give, and when he reemerged for air he dove down again just as quickly. He didn't stay under for as long this time; it felt as though the current had picked up. He reached for a tree root and pulled himself back up onto land. The sound of Alma screaming Tina's name permeated the otherwise silent park. Cayman's soaked clothes weighed him down as he ran to Alma, and the closer he got, the clearer her hysteria, her last shreds of sanity, became. Coming from Alma's mouth, the sound of Tina's name gradually turned into a deafening wail.

Cayman tried to put his arms around his wife. He tried to say Alma's name, to calm her down so they could figure out what happened to their daughter. But at that moment, he may as well have been as disappeared as Tina. He watched Alma dig her fingers into the dirt.

"Where is she?" she cried. "Where *is* she?"

⌒∭⌒

Technically, Cayman wasn't supposed to return to the scene of the disappearance, but at night he could sneak in unnoticed. He'd brought his video camera and a flashlight, though he didn't know what he expected to find. The alligator that he suspected had dragged her into the water while they were napping? Alma hadn't been too fond of that theory.

"That's not how alligators hunt or kill their prey," she'd argued when they were in the hotel waiting for their house to be cleared on that first night of Tina's disappearance.

"What do you know about alligators?" Cayman replied. "You're from Tennessee."

"More than a Cali boy," she'd said. "Don't you think it more likely that she went to the river while we were asleep, misjudged the depth, and was swept under by the current? I'm more prone to believe that a human being stole our daughter while we were asleep than an alligator."

"But I *saw* an alligator," he'd told her. "I felt its tail and saw it slip into the water."

"If it wasn't a trick of the mind," Alma had said, words slurred from tequila, "then it was just a coincidence. No gator took my damn daughter."

Cayman navigated through the darkness of Moss Park's thicket before turning on his camera and switching it to night-vision mode. Even with barely any sleep in over two weeks, operating the camera was second nature to him. He started at the base of the tree where they had napped, the hanging Spanish moss reminiscent of giant spider webs in the darkness, and he made his way toward the overgrowth of yuccas near the river's edge where he'd seen the alligator. He forced his way into the tight-knit spread of tall brush, careful with the camera, his movement smooth as a dolly. He kept his gaze focused on the LCD, the little greens and grays of the night vision mode more true than his own eyesight. Around him, he heard the low choir of crickets and the slow stream of the river, quieter than it had been the day Tina disappeared.

Fifteen minutes passed and, so far as he could tell, he and his camera were the only things that occupied the park. At land's edge, he stopped recording and looked out over the river, the moon's glow reflecting upon its shifting surface. If not for the undying hope that his daughter might one day return, Cayman might have waded out into the water in search of the river's bottom, content to never again return to the surface world. Without Tina, what would happen to him and Alma? He didn't think it likely that they could survive the loss of their daughter, knowing that they'd only been hanging on by a very thin thread since she'd been gone.

Just as he bent down to search for any sign of Tina—a shoe, a shred of her t-shirt—he heard something move nearby in the yucca patch. And a deep, guttural gurgle. A growl.

He flicked his camera back on and hit record, but as soon as he raised it to peer at the LCD he was swept off his feet. His back thudded against the cold ground, the air knocked out of him. He'd felt something strong at his ankles, what must have been the gator's tail. Instinct pulled him off the ground and sent him running away from the river, through the hanging moss and the police tape, until he was back in the garage, heart racing and feeling more alive than ever.

∽∞∽

Cayman returned to Moss Park the following night to find the camera, which must have fallen into the brush when he hit the ground. That day, he decided not to tell Alma about his second encounter with the alligator for fear of starting an argument. She would have just accused him of making matters worse and tampering with the crime scene. He waited for her to fall asleep before he returned, and he left a fresh bottle of Cuervo by the bedside in case she woke up.

It had rained throughout the day, so Cayman worried that the camera would be ruined. When he got to the river, its rapids were quicker than the night before. He used a flashlight to search for the camera and, sure enough, it was right next to the spot where the gator had taken him down. He dislodged it out of the mud and tried to turn it on. No power, no life, which he hoped was only due to a drained battery.

He left the park after fifteen minutes of waiting for the alligator to return. With no sign of movement except for the river, he wondered if there had ever been an alligator at all. There was the slight possibility, as Alma had suggested, that the alligator was only a trick of the mind. Maybe he'd tripped over a root or log before he dropped the camera.

When he returned to the garage, he plugged the camera into an outlet, but the charge light did not illuminate. He wiped away all the mud, pressed all of the buttons. Totally powerless.

He felt a twinge of sentimental loss. The little machine was like an extension of his body, a third eye through which he saw aspects of the world otherwise invisible to the physical laws of human sight. With that camera, he'd caught a bald eagle devouring a marmot in the Rockies, an anhinga in the Everglades gliding across the surface of swamp water with a crayfish in its bill. He remembered, distinctly, the footage of Tina when she was two, smiling widely with a firefly aglow on her finger.

He opened the garage door, sat down on the old couch, and flicked on the television to rewatch the footage of his daughter. Though he couldn't play back the footage through the camera, he could always hook up the HDMI to his laptop. And then he realized—the SD card.

He got up from the couch and rushed over to the camera. He opened the sideguard and pressed down on the card; it sprang into his palm. He held the SD card between his fingers as if it were something rare and fragile, and he inserted it into the side of the laptop. Once the data loaded in the Finder window, he clicked the most recent icon. The footage appeared on the television, and he tapped the spacebar before returning to the couch.

He watched the footage of the park closely in case he'd missed something in person. However, everything looked exactly as he'd remembered it. In the footage, he was seconds away from being taken down. His heart pounded; had the camera shut off when it hit the ground?

The sound of the alligator's growl filled the garage. It didn't last as long as he remembered—perhaps part of the illusion of experiencing the same thing twice. Moments after the growl, sure enough, the images on the screen wobbled incomprehensibly from dropping the camera and, after a loud CLUNK, settled to stillness in the dirt.

Then came the sound of his footsteps, running away from the camera until they were gone. Cayman sat up straight and held his breath. How long did the camera keep rolling? First, he saw and heard leaves rustling. Then an insect landed on the lens. About forty seconds passed when the picture on the screen shook and the insect fled. A moment after that, just out of focus, something new came into the frame, too close to the lens to make out. It hovered in place, occupying the entire screen. Another few seconds passed and the mass moved again, inching toward the right side of the screen until a bright white orb came into view. Another few seconds and the orb went black, then white again. Then Cayman realized. The white orb was an eye. Such that belonged to an alligator.

He nearly ran up to wake Alma when the sight of the alligator exiting the frame stopped him. There came another moment of stillness in the out-of-focus surrounding brush, and then the familiar growls and grunts of the alligator off camera. These sounds, however, were different than the ones earlier in the recording, the ones he'd first heard in person. They were longer in duration. Slower, more pained. Gradually, the rumbling, not so different from that of a small motor, grew higher in pitch, closer to that of a frog. Within another few seconds, the frog-like chirping sounded like a child with strep throat. Next came what Cayman would have bet his life sounded like cries—human ones—and sobs, muffled between attempts at saying "Daddy."

The hairs rose on his arm and neck. The noises stopped, and on the screen, there was only the barely moving brush. Until, for less than a second, there was something—a blur—the figure of a child—running across the screen.

Cayman's forehead was suddenly moist, feverish. He pressed the reverse key on the keyboard and paused when the blur was directly in the center of the screen. The figure was, undoubtedly, that of a person. The size of a toddler. In the still frame on the screen, the figure's eyes were as white as the orb of the gator's earlier in the footage, and they were looking directly into the camera.

"Alma," Cayman muttered, throat dry. He ran for the door, stumbling over the couch. He rushed upstairs to the bedroom and shouted his wife's name, jolting her from a sound sleep.

"Tina," he cried. "Our girl. Come quick."

Alma's dumbfounded glare did not immediately register his words, so he said, much louder, "Our *daughter*. TINA. *Come now*." He leapt down the stairs and swung open the door to the garage, but the television screen was blue again.

And the laptop was gone.

"No," Cayman said. He darted over to the stand where the laptop had been but moments ago and shouted, "*No, no, NO!*" There were droplets of water on the stand's woodgrain surface. He turned to see a trail of droplets getting bigger—puddles— leading to the wide-open mouth of the garage door.

"What the hell is the big idea?"

Cayman spun around to see Alma standing in her robe in the doorframe.

"She was here," he said. "Well, not *here*. On the TV. First, it was the gator from the other night. And then it was her. She said 'Daddy,' Al. She saw me and said 'Daddy,' but..."

He looked back to the puddles of water and followed them beyond the garage door, where outside it had started to drizzle. He scanned the yard and driveway, and then he ran out into the street.

He screamed, "*Hey!*"

Nothing but stillness all around him.

"*HEY!*"

Across the street, the neighbor's living room light flicked on.

"Was it you?" Cayman yelled to the neighbor. "You come into my garage and steal my laptop?"

The neighbor stood still in the window.

A few more lights illuminated in nearby houses.

Cayman was prepared to make a spectacle of his rage. Blood coursing quickly through his veins, clothing soaked, he wanted the neighbors—he wanted God—to know the wrath of which his daughter's disappearance made him capable.

"Cay," Alma said from behind him, her voice soothing, sweet. "We've got to stop this now. Okay? It's done. It's over." She took him by the hand and led him inside, past the puddles, to the couch. She pressed the button to close the garage door and joined him on the sunken-down cushions where they held each other, the mechanical sound of the garage-mouth muting Cayman's cries until the room was swallowed in darkness.

෨෩෨

The next morning, while still in the darkness of the garage, Alma told him she was leaving.

"I know you blame me," he said. "For not watching her close enough. I blame myself. But you don't have to go, Al. Don't go."

"I can't argue," she said. "I just need space. For a little while."

That night she took a flight from Tampa to Nashville. She never once offered the chance for him to go with her. Never once told him to leave Florida for Tennessee or California. But she knew as well as he did that leaving Tampa was something he could not do. Not yet.

෨ා‏

Cayman barely slept after that. Time had passed, but it no longer mattered how much. He thought about selling the house, but he couldn't let go of the idea that one day Tina would return and he wouldn't be there. While he could no longer commit to his role as producer at Bay News, the station kept him on staff as an independent contractor, and he edited footage from home so he could pay down the mortgage. He set up an editing station in the garage, where he also slept and took his meals and waited. Sometime after Alma left, the foundation that had provided him the grant to create his series about metamorphoses inquired about the status of the project. Admittedly, the series had taken a backseat when Tina was born. However, since Alma left, Cayman had spent his seemingly incessant waking hours working on the series when he wasn't editing for the news station. Including the footage from Butterfly World, the series contained nearly a dozen segments focused on the transformation of tadpoles to frogs, the life cycle of dragon-flies from egg to nymph to adult, the four-stage cycle of the white grub to beetle, the nine-month cycle of human growth in the womb, and an incomplete segment about unexplainable metamorphoses.

The footage he had spliced of the alligator that swept him off his feet and the figure of what he believed to be his daughter could hardly be considered scientific data. He was sure he'd be laughed at by members of the grant foundation, who would also strongly advise him to omit the final segment from what would otherwise be considered a moving and scholarly series.

Unless he could prove his theory with more footage.

Cayman returned to Moss Park with a new camera several times. He'd often stay until dawn, filling up multiple SD cards in hope of new evidence. He'd even stationed cameras in the garage and left them rolling when he wasn't home, but he did not see the alligator or the toddler-sized figure again.

One morning, after hours of filming, Cayman stumbled into a bar in Seminole Heights called Hole in the Wall. The sun had not yet come up, and the only other patron at that hour was a tall, dark-skinned man with gray hair in a long braid. Cayman sat a few seats away from him and ordered a beer.

"I recognize you," the man said. He got up and moved closer to Cayman. "Your face. From the news. When your little girl disappeared."

Cayman nodded and sucked his teeth. This close, Cayman could see the deep wrinkles in the man's face.

"You're not from here," the man continued. "This place, it's not welcoming. Too much blood in the soil."

Cayman wondered how much the man had already had to drink.

"Are you from here?" he asked the man.

He nodded. "A descendant of the Seminole tribe."

The man ordered two shots of Cuervo, which made Cayman miss Alma.

"To those who are lost," the man said. "May they one day be found."

Cayman clinked his shot glass against the man's. They each downed the tequila, and Cayman welcomed the burn.

"Bring the bottle," the man called to the bartender.

Later, once the bottle was nearly empty, Cayman smiled and said, "I've lost so much sleep that I can't tell what's real anymore. I don't even know if you're real." He looked to the bartender. "Is this guy real?"

The bartender gave a disinterested nod.

"Tell me everything," the man said. "I'll help you decide what's real."

Cayman swallowed and wiped the tequila from his mouth.

"An alligator came up out of the river and dragged my daughter into the water," he said, the buzz helping to suppress the tears. "And then my little girl turned into one. An alligator. Came back home, after all. But she took the only evidence I had. What else would have left those puddles behind? Must not have wanted her old life anymore." Being drunk made him feel less stupid saying it out loud. "I know I sound crazy. Like I lost my damn mind. Alma thinks I did. Maybe it's true."

The man stared at Cayman, seemingly unfazed by the drink.

"A long time ago, many of my people were killed here. The rest were forced out of this land. Our home. But the Seminole name remains, as do the souls of my ancestors. For the Seminole, the alligator is sacred. There is a tale, some might call it legend, of the letiche."

Cayman clenched his jaw, eager for the man to continue.

"As legend has it, there was once a child who got lost by the river and cried for his parents for hours. The parents looked everywhere but never found the child. That night, an alligator mother heard the child's cries. The child did not know to be afraid of the alligator, and so it followed her when she asked to take it back to her home. Down in the alligator's den, there is said to be an ancient magic. The alligator mother brought the child to her den, and as the child slept, it grew a tail and snout and woke as an alligator. It lived the rest of its life happily, though it would seldomly return to its old form and search the land for its parents."

The man lit a cigar and flipped his shot glass upside down.

"So, what happened?" asked Cayman. "Did the child ever finds its parents?"

The man exhaled a cloud of smoke. Cayman heard a soft roll of thunder outside.

"Yes, it found its parents," the man said. "But it did not return to them, because by then it was already grown. It no longer had any memory of their love."

Cayman inhaled deeply. He stood from the bar, tapped the counter twice as if to tell the man goodbye, and walked outside to wait for the rain.

And he let the rain wash over him.

Property Damage

*E*ver since I caught Lorraine with another man, there's been a lot of good property on the market, which has kept my mind off the whole thing. I figure a couple more years of remodeling these on-campus houses and I'll be working on those nice, three-story brick jobs out in Perrysburg and Sylvania, sitting by the edge of the Maumee River.

A big part of being a property owner is building a network of clientele. Hell, lately it hasn't even been about the money. I'm happy just doing good in west Toledo, helping out my neighbors with their drywall or putting in new driveways. The way I see it, I'm going to need to know all this stuff if I'm ever going to be successful in this business.

I don't even mind rolling out of bed at eight in the morning to help Ms. Engleson, who lives two blocks over, with the pipes flooding her basement. I throw on an extra button-up shirt and scarf to combat the late-October wind chill, and I'm out the door. On these brisk, sharp mornings, I don't even want to take the car—I'd rather just walk the two blocks, admiring architecture while putzing around the neighborhood.

I take my time walking, admiring the houses on my street—mostly all copies of one another with a slight variation in the design of the front porch or a balcony on the second level. I don't have to be to my sister's for her "mock therapy session" for another couple hours, so on my way over to see Ms. Engleson about her basement pipes, I stop at the one interesting house on my street, an old Victorian building that's been up for a hundred years or so, like the ones down in the Old West End. I wish the houses were still like that in this neighborhood, instead of dingy replicas meant to be rebuilt after two years of abuse from a new batch of college partiers. But I can't deny that their need for cheap housing is what keeps me in business, so I try to take pleasure in nursing a property back to health for the next round.

The Victorian house has been occupied by the Rayners for as long as I can remember, an old Korean couple who I'm pretty sure is filthy rich because Mr. Rayner is always driving around in a new Cadillac and, sure enough, a few months later he's got a better one. This month, it's a fire-red S700 with chrome rims. Last time Mr. Rayner caught me measuring his siding, he talked my ear off about the entire purpose of his investments in the automobile industry.

"Years of hard work led to the luxury of a new vehicle whenever I so desired," he said. "I know a man I could put you in touch with if you're ever interested in a position at the factory. They offer a great health package."

All of this sounded attractive at the time because, at that point, I was still getting married to Lorraine, and she hadn't fucked Demetrius Ollerton on the mattress I bought, on the bed frame I made for her during our sophomore year of college. Back then I thought maybe finding something a little more steady with insurance benefits would be a better choice for the long term.

When I get to the Rayners' veranda, I take the tape measure out of my back pocket and measure the paneling. I write the measurements down in my pocketbook. Lorraine always pointed out the Rayners' veranda and would say things like, "One day, Mark, we'll have a veranda like that and we can just sit out, read, and drink lemonade." Even without Lorraine, I figure I'd be a fool to think that I can't enjoy sitting out, reading, or drinking lemonade by myself or with anyone else on a veranda I put together with my own two hands.

From the corner of my eye, I see Mr. Rayner through the window of his house. He's stark naked, frantically waving for me to leave. I feel bad for embarrassing the poor guy, so I hurry back to the sidewalk and continue to Ms. Engleson's.

I don't even have to knock on Ms. Engleson's door. As soon as I walk up the creaky, wooden steps, she opens it up like she's been watching out the window for me this whole time. For a woman in her mid-40s, I always thought Ms. Engleson was attractive enough, and other men must have thought so, too, because for a stretch of years it seemed like there were always different cars parked in her driveway, none of them her own. Standing there with the door open, she's wearing a long, embroidered bathrobe and her hair is done up in fresh curls, and there's a light shade of blue painted above each eyelid's black stripe.

"Good morning, Ms. Engleson," I say.

"Mark," she says, smiling and tilting one knee inward, "for the thousandth time, you of all people can call me Nell."

"Right," I say. "Nell, how bad are the pipes looking?"

"Oh, god, I almost forgot," she says, leading me inside. "The whole basement floor is damn near underwater." I close the door behind me and follow Ms. Engleson down to the basement, where a small layer of water is growing under a fountain erupting from the pipes.

"To tell you the truth, Ms. Engleson—er, Nell—a leak like this is out of my league. It might be a better idea to call a professional plumber."

She puts her hand on my arm. "I can't afford a professional plumber right now. That would run three, maybe four hundred dollars. Plus, didn't you say you were trying to learn everything there was to know about the workings of a house?"

She has me there. I did say that, and have been telling everyone in the neighborhood since the incident. I had to prove to everyone I wasn't a bad guy even though I lit a mattress and bed frame on fire on the front lawn, that I was still serious about my business endeavors, and wanted to be a good neighbor and contribute to my community. After all, I did put out the fire with the hydrant across the street. Everyone saw me put it out—Zoe saw me put it out, Sam saw me put it out, Lorraine and her parents and her little sister saw me put it out, and most of the neighborhood, including Ms. Engleson, saw me put it out. That's why it is my destiny to fix her pipes. I've become the neighborhood handyman. I can't have my community thinking I'm crazy or something.

After running back home to get a set of wrenches, and running all the way past the Rayners' to Ms. Engleson's again, I spend about two hours on the pipes, hacking away with an old hand saw and trying to connect the ends of the metal and lead until finally the leaking stops, with only three inches of water to bucket out of the basement.

"Well, it's not a perfect fix, but it'll do for now." I look at my watch, a quarter before noon, and realize I'm about to be running late for Zoe's therapy session.

"I knew you could do it," she says, her hand on my arm again. I swear I feel her bare foot graze mine under the small pond of water. "I can't imagine what woman would be foolish enough to search beyond you. As far as I can tell, you're the perfect man."

"I'm running late, Nell," I say as I start to head for the stairs. "But I think the pipes will hold up for now."

"Maybe you could stay and help me with all this water," she says. "I could really use your help, Mark." The light layer of blue from her eyes drips down her cheekbones from the splash of the pipes' current. She looks like a crying cartoon character as she leans into me. She tries to dry her face on my shirt, but I run up the stairs before she gets to me.

"I'll check back tomorrow, Ms. Engleson."

"Don't forget, young man," I hear her yell from all the way outside. "And it would do you well to stop being so damn polite all the time."

❦

On the way over to Zoe's, I can't help but drive over the speed limit. The last thing I need is my little sister, who has a chip on her shoulder from the psychology classes she's taking at the university, to tell me how I need to shape up. I can just hear her now.

It's been over a month, Mark.

You used to be so different, Mark.

I can't believe you're late—I was counting on you.

I pull up five after and she's already out in front of her dorm, smoking a cigarette, staring at my car and shaking her head.

"Please don't start," I say.

"Who was it this time?"

"Ms. Engleson needed her pipes fixed."

She takes a drag of the cigarette, cracking a smile. "I'll bet she did."

"There's about three feet of water in her basement. I need to get back to help her dry it out before it causes property damage."

"Well, let's get started then." She puts out her cigarette against the stone siding of the stairwell and enters the apartment without holding the door for me.

When I get inside, she has her La-Z-Boy sitting perpendicular to the futon, which is folded out, half-covered with pillows, to look like a therapy session and everything.

"You went all out," I say.

"This is the professional way to go about it."

"You know, you never give Sam a hard time about being late."

I'm distracted by a fly buzzing around an old can of soda stuffed with cigarette ashes.

"Sam's the baby," she says, taking notes.

I sit down on the futon. "What's that have to do with anything?"

"You're the eldest."

"So why does the burden of punctuality have to fall on me?"

"Because you're our big brother. You're supposed to set the example."

"I call bullshit."

"Do you want to talk about your sibling relationship? We can, if that's what you'd like. We have one hour, starting one and a half minutes ago. I figured you'd want to talk about Lorraine, but we can talk about—"

"Why do you assume I want to talk about Lorraine?" I interrupt, sitting parallel to her, not looking at her, and swat at the fly that keeps buzzing around my face.

"Because your whole reality is broken due to your fiancée cheating on you."

"Excuse me? My reality is broken?" I look over to the textbook she has opened on the side table and try to find anything about broken realities. All I see are big, complex, and colorful diagrams, a blue and purple one of the human brain, and a red and orange one of the human heart. If I could only crush the fly smack in the middle, I might actually be able to think straight.

"I'm sorry," she says. "Forget I said anything. We can talk about whatever you want."

I stretch my legs out across the futon, putting my back against the pillows with Zoe behind me, jotting away.

"'Broken reality' just sounds like a really harsh phrase. I don't know if I'd go as far as to say that my reality is broken, but yeah, something definitely feels off."

"Off," she says. "What do you mean, 'off'?"

"You know, like one day everything was one way and now it's a different way."

"Would you say that it's better or worse?"

"Worse," I spit out, as if there is any possibility of me enjoying a life where I can't see Lorraine every day. Where there is no five years of courting. Dates. Lovemaking. Studying. Day trips. Dinners. Wedding plans. Graduating college together. Supporting Lorraine while she went back to school for her master's. Me working hard to expand the business. Establishing a good home for her where we could spend the rest of our lives once she finished school. Where we could raise children and have our friends over for cookouts in the back yard. On the veranda. Where afterward we'd drink lemonade. Read while the sun went down.

"Much worse." I half-want to ask Zoe for a cigarette even though I haven't had one since the carton I chain-smoked on the night of the incident.

"Do you feel like your mind continues to wander to the past?"

"Yes, of course it wanders to the past. Isn't that natural?"

"What parts of the past specifically?"

"Are you asking me if I think about the incident still?"

"Do you think about the incident still?"

I'm starting to wonder if Zoe even needs to do this for a class or if she's just trying to get me to talk about things, like always. It's no secret she gets a high from figuring out every little microscopic thing about people and trying to understand how things like falling off the swings when you're three is related to motion sickness on a sailboat when you're twenty-two.

"You know I do."

"Have you ever heard of retroactive thinking?"

"You know I haven't."

"Retroactive thinking is when you let your mind tread over traumatic incidents or events in your life. It is common to get caught in retroactive thinking, especially right after an incident like the one you went through, Mark. But if you are able to realize early that your mind is caught in a web of venomous thoughts, then you may have a chance of escaping further trauma. You don't want your episodic memory to deteriorate."

"I get it. You're saying that I have to stop thinking about the incident. And anything else that ever caused me pain."

"That's not what I'm saying. I don't think you're quite seeing the point. I'm going to ask you to do something for me, and doing what I ask will help alleviate any retroactive thinking and put the painful memories of the incident at rest. It's kind of like the theory that if you write down your painful feelings or memories and burn the paper, then those feelings and memories burn away with it."

"You know I'm the one who taught you how to burn away emotions," I say.

"No, you didn't. I read it in Nabokov. Maybe Bukowski."

"I was seven and you were four. It was right after we lost Muffy."

"Mark, you're not making much sense right now."

"Heaven forbid I ever say anything that makes sense."

She exhales, takes a cigarette from her pack, places it in her mouth and takes it back out, only to sheathe it back in the pack.

"I'm trying to ask you to do something very specific for me here, Mark."

"What are you going to ask me to do?"

"I would like you to very carefully, very idiosyncratically, give me a moment by moment, detail by detail account of the incident.

I swallow hard. I should have known this was coming. "Zoe, I think maybe we should refocus to childhood or something, like Muffy—"

"If you ignore it, it's only going to grow and fester and, one day, it's going to swallow you whole." Without looking at her, I can tell her eyes are glued to the back of my head like this is the most dire request she's ever made in her life.

"What do you want me to say, Zoe? You know what happened. One morning I have an appointment with some potential buyers on the Delaney Street property, and you know how hard I've been trying to flip that one, so it's a big deal. I tell Lorraine I'm not going to be able to get her lunch today because it's a Tuesday, so she has a break between noon and one thirty. I always get her lunch on Tuesdays and Thursdays, but not this Tuesday because of the appointment for the Delaney Street property. But I get all the way out to the property and find a note from the buyers saying they have to cancel until next week, and I'm really bummed because that property goes for forty thousand, but at the same time, I'm excited because I still get to get lunch for Lorraine—"

All of a sudden my throat gets dry and I cough, trying to hack some phlegm out of my throat, praying it's not the fly, and before I know it, I swallow the phlegm down again, which I know Zoe hates, but I know she'd also hate it if I got up to spit it out.

"Do you realize what you're doing?" she says, handing me a packet of tissues.

"I'm giving you a step-by-step account of what happened," I say.

"No, you are giving me a step-by-step account of what is happening. You are telling the story in the present tense. You always tell the story in the present tense."

I laugh. "What the hell has that got to do with anything?"

"It has to do with the fact that, in your head, you think of the incident and you replay it in live action. You still retain the memory as if it's in the present, as if the consequences haven't even happened yet. What you need to do is release the story by telling it in the past tense, which will put it behind you once and for all."

I turn to look back at her, and as I knew would happen, she's tearing up just like when we were kids and I refused to talk about my feelings after our cat, Muffy, was crushed by one of Mr. Rayner's Cadillacs. It's the same look she wore when we stood in the backyard saying our last words to the casket. The same look as when I cried and told her, Sam, mom, dad, and Muffy's ghost that Muffy was my first and closest friend.

I had said, "Never in my whole seven years of life did I know a person could be this sad." And just as I broke down in tears then, I close my eyes and break down again now.

⌘

It was the hottest day of August, and I woke up early to see Lorraine before her first class, and, as always, I took her a peppermint latte because that's how she liked to start her day before all that studying. It was an iced peppermint latte due to the heat. She wore her short pink cottons. Her legs weren't exactly hairy, but they weren't exactly smooth, either. I still thought she was the sexiest woman I'd ever see in my life. The water dripped from the plastic cup onto her thighs and then ran down her ankles. She dabbed her fingertip in the water and spread it around her leg.

"I can put an air conditioner in here," I said. I had been telling her all summer that the heat wouldn't let off anytime soon, that it was no trouble to put in a small window unit. Anything for her.

"They always distract me when they're running. Besides," she laughed, sipping the last of the latte, "I think I study better when I'm all sweaty."

As she bit at her straw, I told her all about the appointment with the buyers for the Delaney Street property, and that if it sold, I could finally afford to build the walk-in closet I designed for her. I bought the house the summer after we finished our undergraduate programs, but Lorraine only had the summer before she'd have to be back to get the master's. She had two more years, but the plan was to have the house finished and perfected so when she was all graduated and we were married, we could finally relax and enjoy our time together.

"I hope it goes through," she said. She took her shirt off and sat there in her bra with the sweat building between her breasts. "But I'd really better get to work."

I kissed her on the forehead and rushed out the door, realizing I was already running late to meet the buyers. I cruised down River Road as fast as I could, and, with the windows down, I couldn't help but gaze at the river and the way the sun beamed off its calm surface. I managed to get to the property right on time, only to find the entire trip was pointless because the buyers had already been to the property and left a note taped to the door saying how something came up, a family emergency, and they'd still look at the property the following week. I didn't get too bent up about it because I'd still have forty-five minutes with Lorraine if I could get to her in time. On the way back, I stopped at Zingo's to pick up a vegan gyro—Lorraine's favorite—so she'd be well-fed for her night classes.

By the time I got back to the apartment, I still had fifteen minutes before Lorraine had to leave. However, as I pulled around the corner, I was alarmed at first to see a car in my usual spot. I figured it was no problem, that I'd just pull to the side, put my hazards on, and walk the vegan gyro up to Lorraine, kiss her on the cheek, tell her to have a good night, and I'd be waiting for her to get out.

But after I unlocked the top latch, I turned the handle, and it was locked.

She never locks the handle, I thought. Maybe she's taking a shower.

That had to be it. She was just paranoid to be alone in the shower. She wanted to make sure the door was extra safe. The vehicle in my spot had Georgia plates. I didn't know anyone in the area from Georgia.

The key to the door handle was different than the key to the deadbolt. This fact, I've discerned, is what gave Demetrius enough time to get off Lorraine before I got to the bed. I stared at them for a good fifteen seconds before I fully comprehended that it was Demetrius' car in my spot. It took a full fifteen seconds of viewing Demetrius' sweat-soaked, naked body shielding Lorraine's sweat-soaked, naked body for me to restrain myself from killing him.

"What the fuck is going on, Lorraine?" I asked, the keys clenched in my fist.

"I—I thought you would be gone."

Demetrius tried to guard himself and Lorraine from me by putting his hand up, firm and steady.

"Look, Mark," he said, "if you can just give me one minute, I'll get my clothes on and be out of here. There's no need to—"

I plowed through Demetrius, shoving him aside so I wouldn't have to touch or look at Lorraine.

In that lava-hot room, I believed our collision would cause spontaneous combustion.

From there, everything gets a little hazy. I remember some-one's hands were clawing at me. And that I ripped the sheets off the mattress before dragging it through the bedroom doorframe and into the living room. That's when I knocked over the TV and the coatrack. Before I took the mattress out onto the front lawn of the apartment complex, I remember feeling baffled by the silence of the room—no lungs breathing. No clocks ticking. No fans blowing. Just Lorraine, her eyes fixed on me, mouth agape. Demetrius lay on the floor, holding his swollen face. The apartment breathed this hot, foul air. It had a pulse, like some ancient quag regurgitating the mattress and me from its acidic bowels.

Once I had the mattress out the front door, it was no trouble getting it down the stairs, even with Lorraine running after me in her big t-shirt that hung above her kneecaps.

"Give back Demetrius' car keys," she wailed. "Please just come back inside."

First, I tossed the keys into a nearby sewer grate.

And then I went back inside, all right.

To retrieve the bed frame I'd built with my bare hands.

Because I'd fall dead before I let another man continue to sleep with my fiancée atop it.

Lorraine leaped away as I trudged back in. When Demetrius saw me coming, he was partially knelt down, pulling his underwear over his loins. I lunged toward him with my fist pulled back, simply to make him flinch at the force my rage had become. As he cowered, I flipped the bed frame on its side, pulled it through the apartment and past Lorraine, and hurled it into the yard like an Olympic discus thrower.

I arranged the mattress back into position on the bedframe and went for the gas can.

That's when I noticed them.

Sometime between tossing Demetrius' keys in the sewer's mouth and retrieving the gas can from my trunk, the neighbors started to see something was happening outside and, go figure, they all crowded around like it was a community cookout. It must have been the fact that I was raising my voice, but since Lorraine kept telling me to "please be quiet, come back inside, don't do this, please, I'm begging you, it was a mistake," I just kept saying louder and louder, "I have to light this mattress and bed frame on fire. Don't you see? Don't you see, Lorraine? This mattress is no good anymore. It must be burned. And the bed frame I made with my bare hands must also burn by my hand!" I must have been screaming because, to be honest, I believed Lorraine couldn't hear me.

As I poured the gasoline over the mattress and bed frame, I didn't think anything of the neighbors, creating a perimeter around me, hands over their mouths, some with their phones out, hesitant to call the cops. I knew they wouldn't, though. I knew they would just stand there and watch, because they knew me, every one of them. Mr. Abernath, who told me stories about the war when I helped with the hardwood floors in his kitchen. Little Bobby and Trina Fischer, who played every day on the swing set I helped their father install in their backyard. Ray-Ray Stevens, who taught me how to single-handedly wire an entire heating system in a two-floor unit. Margot Lundgren, whose porch I fixed to accommodate a ramp when she broke her leg.

The entire block, I'd say, all crowded around me. Not one of them said a word when I struck the match and tossed it onto the mattress, or when the flames shot up in one barbarous gust, followed by the blanket of smoke that danced up to the sky. Not even Lorraine, or Demetrius—standing there in one of

Lorraine's bath towels—muttered a single word as I fed the fire with more gasoline until the can was empty. I threw the can to the ground and turned around, making a rush to the car. The neighbors cleared a path, like Moses parting the waters, for me to get the wrench from my car, stomp over to the sidewalk, and apply the wrench to the fire hydrant. For a second, I felt like King Arthur pulling Excalibur out of the stone—clutching the wrench with all my might—until finally, like a torrent bursting through the fractured walls of a dam, the hydrant released its power, as if by magic, directly onto the flaming mattress. Steam devoured the air like fog, with only the silhouettes of people visible. Apparitions in a dense haze.

⟆⟇⟆⟇⟆

At this point I'm pacing around the apartment, and I've even smoked one or two of Zoe's cigarettes down to the filter. She's telling me to calm down, that I shouldn't be ashamed of crying, and all the stuff I'm sure they teach her to say in her psychology classes. The fact of the matter is that all this retroactive thinking has me wondering for the first time since the incident why the hell I never went back to Lorraine after that day. By now Demetrius probably has his grubby Georgia furniture littering the apartment, having to pick up all of Lorraine's panties from hanging over it just to watch them pile in a corner. I can't get the thought out of my head—their sweaty bodies touching, their minds indulging. All I can think about is driving over to the apartment to see Lorraine and figure out once and for all what happened and why.

Zoe tries to stop me going to the car. "You shouldn't drive if you're having an anxiety attack," she says. "I have to go to class soon. You can just hang out here for a while."

"I have to see Lorraine," I say.

"No," she says, "that's the last thing you should do."

But I'm already in the car speeding away from Zoe's dorm and toward Lorraine's apartment.

There's some pop song on the radio, the one about the guy telling the girl that all he wants is for her to say how she wants him, and that she'll always be there forever, and I know all the words, so I crank up the volume, roll the windows down, and belt it out for the world to hear.

By the time I get to the apartment, I see from across the lot that the door is open and there's a big For Rent sign out front. It has barely been a month, and Lorraine's gone and moved in with Demetrius. And after all that crap about not wanting to stay in the house with me because there always seemed like there was so much to do. Her excuse was that she could think by herself now that we weren't both in college together. She promised she would live in the house once she graduated.

I park the car and don't even bother turning it off or putting the hazards on or closing the door. I just step out and sprint across the grass and leap over the giant yellow spot where the mattress burned. Once I'm inside, I play it cool like a cop in one of those movies where they go to search the place—I point my hand out like a gun and everything, checking each corner twice, until I'm certain the place is empty, and then I drop to my knees and chew the collar of my shirt and cry until all the snot drains out of my face.

It feels weird leaving the door open with the place all empty like this, so I lock the door, close it, and take the For Rent sign out of the ground. I throw the sign in my trunk and drive off. I can't imagine where Lorraine managed to run off to, but I do know if there's anyone who could tell me her whereabouts, it's her family.

I head a few miles east across the High Level Bridge to her parents' place because I have to assume her mom, her dad, or her sister will have the decency to fill me in on the situation. I circle their block three times, triple-checking for Lorraine's car, or Demetrius' car, or Lorraine's sister, Claire, walking around the block with her friends. After the third time, I figure it starts to look pretty sketchy, me driving around and around, and I can't even possess myself to stop the car, go up to her parents' house, and ask about her because, truth be told, I don't know what I'll do if I see her. The whole spontaneous combustion thing.

Now, things normally don't go sour for me, but when they do, I always feel better when I go back to campus. I guess something about the big limestone buildings and, this season, the dead leaves on the ground, remind me of a time when everything was simpler. Back then, everything was so fresh with Lorraine and every day felt so new. First it was kissing. Then sex. Then picking a college. Then prom. Then high school graduation. Going to college. Moving in together. Proposing. Keeping it steady until college graduation. Buying the house. Fixing it up. And marriage. We were still looking forward to marriage. At least I was. I even sat her father down and asked for Lorraine's hand.

"I can't imagine my life without her," I had told him. "No matter what, I'll protect her until the day I die."

He'd clasped my hand in his. "Mark," he said, "I always knew you'd be a fine man for my daughter." We hugged each other. The next day I proposed to Lorraine at the giant angel fountain by the Student Union.

Of course, she said yes, and of course I picked her up and kissed her and we spun around. We skipped our classes and made love all that day and all that night. When we came together, we talked about children. In the moonlight, Lorraine's naked body atop mine, she did in fact look into my eyes and confess she believed in eternity. That I was her soul mate. That nothing on this earth could take her away from me. And, goddamnit, I believed her.

Campus is empty because it's a Sunday and bitter cold. I leave my car in the parking lot, the only car there, as I stroll around for an hour or two. I pass the library and Union Fountain and the Annex and the Geology building. When I get back to the car, I sit inside with the seat back and scan the radio for the song about the guy wanting the girl to say she loves him.

After about twenty minutes of searching, I find it and crank it up again and cry it out until my voice is hoarse. I used to come here every Wednesday night because Lorraine had a late Societal Issues class. I'd wait for her here, listen to some music, walk around, grab a bite from the Union, and sit on the hood of the car watching the sun go down and the sky change colors.

Right around sunset, across the parking lot outside this small, brick chapel building, people would stand and walk around on their tiptoes, arms and hands outstretched as if feeling for some imaginary fishing wire descended from the sky. Their patterns seemed random. Sometimes they would walk in long lines outside the small chapel, other times they would gravitate about aimlessly and, somehow, miraculously, never bump into each other. The sign on the door said Campus Diamond Sangha, and after a couple of weeks of watching them orbit the lawn outside the chapel, I decided to do some research and figure out what they were doing.

As it turned out, it was called walking meditation, and Wednesday night was the only night they did it. Most of the other days it was regular meditation, I guess, or group meditation. Sometimes when I sat out in my car on Wednesdays waiting for Lorraine to get out of Societal Issues, I'd think about joining them. The most courage I ever gathered was only enough to walk up to the door and grab a small pamphlet that described what the Sangha was all about.

Of course, the first time I ever think I've got enough gusto to get out there and meditate-walk with the rest of them, there's not a soul in sight. It doesn't stop me from walking over there to see if anyone's inside the chapel. I press my face against the window, and even though the lights are off, I wonder if maybe there's a clerk volunteering at the front desk just in case someone calls the Sangha for information. You never know. I notice there are no more pamphlets out front, and I go for the door handle. Oddly enough, it opens and I find myself inside. There's nobody at the desk, but I see one pair of sandals on a little bamboo matt.

"Hello?" I say. "Is anyone around?"

"Turner?" a soft, scratchy voice says. "Is that you?"

"Uh—No, sorry," I say. "I just kind of wandered in." I look around for where the voice is coming from, but I'm convinced the room is empty until I see someone rounding the corner in a red motorcycle helmet and denim jacket. I almost jump at the sight.

He takes off the shiny helmet to reveal a balding head and grey-blue eyes like crystal. His face is calm yet wrinkled. I imagine an aged baby.

"Didn't mean to frighten you," he says. "I'm Zen Master Seight." He extends his hand to shake, and I take it because

I recognize the name from the pamphlet as the owner of the Sangha. "How may I help you?"

I tighten my grip and say, "I was just walking by. Admiring the property. Thought I'd stop in to see what goes into a building like this. I'm in the business, you see."

"Are you an architect?" he asks. "Or are you a monk?"

"Neither," I say, even though I consider telling him about my designs for the house. "I'm in the property business. I flip property, make it livable, beautiful, and ready for people to be happy in."

"That sounds like a tough business," he says.

"Not that tough at all, actually. I love it. I was wondering, in a place like this where there's a lot of—er—meditation going on, the rooms probably require a certain design. I wasn't sure if the windows need to face a certain direction to align with the sun, or—"

"You can meditate anywhere," the Zen master says, "as long as your mind is in the right place." He sticks his bare big toe into the carpet and rotates his leg as if trying to drill a hole into the ground.

"Right. Of course." And for some reason—it must be my oblong reflection staring back at me off his motorcycle helmet— I think of Lorraine in ten years with someone else's children, and shivers run up my back, through my throat. I start to choke.

"Thank you for your time," I say, scrambling for a business card to give him. All I find is an old, beat up one that's half torn, but I hand it to him anyway and say, "Give me a call. I'd love to talk prices." I'm not sure what I mean by 'talk prices,' but I try to sound convincing because I want him to know I'm serious about all this. As I walk out the door, he sort of bows to me with his palms pressed together and mutters something in another language. I don't need to know what he's saying to understand it means something peaceful.

ᏟᎳᎳᎧ

Parked on Lorraine's parents' street, I rehearse everything I'm going to say once I get to the door. Hello, Mr. or Mrs. Wagner. I don't want to take up too much of your time, but I was just wondering if you know the best way I could get in touch with Lorraine so we can sort everything out. I go over it about a hundred times until, finally, I get out of the car, walk up to the door, and ring the bell. Go figure, it's Claire, who's gotten taller since the last time I saw her, unusually tall for a twelve-year-old. She's looking at me like I'm on some Wanted poster all over town.

"Uh, hi, Claire. Is your sister around?"

"You shouldn't be here, Mark," she says, blowing a fat, blue bubblegum bubble. "Please just go. You don't want to see her."

I try to peer in through the screen door. "What do you mean? Why not? Is she in there right now?"

She says, "I'm sorry, Mark," and closes the door softly in my face. I don't know whether to go back to the car or to try again, but before I can make a decision, the door opens and I expect to see Claire. But it's Lorraine looking at me, and even through the screen, I can see the tears welling in her eyes.

Before I can catch myself, my hand extends out, reaching for her face, but my fingers touch the screen and get a black residue on the tips.

"Lorraine," I say. "I just needed to see you."

"I told you not to come around, Mark," she says.

I laugh because she knows damn well she never said that to me.

"Are you still wearing the ring?" I ask, half-expecting her to raise her hand up for me to see through the screen, the ring right there on her finger, as if to say, "What do you think, silly?"

But I know better. I know the ring may as well be at the bottom of the ocean.

"Now's not a good time," she says.

"You were supposed to be my wife. How could you, Lorraine?"

"I don't know what to say. I just can't do this. It's too much right now."

I go for the screen door handle, but she jumps rabbit-quick to the latch, and I'm left looking crazy as the metal door bangs from my failed attempt at opening it.

"Just come talk to me. We can go anywhere. I can't think. I can't breathe. I can't eat."

"Yes, you can, Mark. Just go home." And then she, too, closes the door in my face.

But I know her.

I'm willing to bet this is some kind of test.

I plop down on the steps in front of the screen door, biting my nails until the door opens again.

I jump up, but this time it's Mr. Wagner.

"Hey, Mr. Wagner, I'm sorry about the misunderstanding."

"There is no misunderstanding, Mark," he says. "I need you to get off my property, or I'll have no choice but to call the cops."

I'm as speechless as the time he caught Lorraine and me during senior year fooling around on top of their basement billiards table.

"Mr. Wagner, I—"

"Please, Mark," he says. "Don't make this harder than it has to be." I think I catch a look of regret on his face, maybe even an apology, before he closes the door. I can see Mrs. Wagner and Claire watching me from behind the curtain of the living room window. Next thing I know, I catch glimpses from a few of the neighbors behind their own curtains. I guarantee they're all expecting a show.

They heard all about the last one.

And I'd love to give it to them, too.

I'd love to spell Lorraine's name out in gasoline, right in the street, and strike a match so she can see my love for her blazing bright.

I've never so much as set off a firecracker on the Fourth of July, but ever since the incident, if I'm thinking of Lorraine, chances are I'm also thinking of fire, because that's what she feels like inside my head. Inside my heart. My blood. But despite the flame coursing through my veins, I stop myself from giving them something to watch. I refuse to be something they talk about until Christmas.

Instead, I make the only rational decision: go back to my car, drive to the Cash N' Save for a fifth of whiskey, and return to the house. Once inside, I crack open the bottle, take a big swig, and play back the messages from the day.

"Hey, Mark, it's me, Nell. I just had a quick question for you—should I wait for you to drain the water from the basement? Give me a call, hon'."

"Hi, Mark, this is Mr. Rayner from down the street. Yeah, I'd really appreciate it if you'd please stay out of my yard. I'd be happy to discuss any dimensions or measurements you may need over the phone, at a reasonable hour. Don't forget about the opening I told you about at the factory. Give my buddy Jed a call."

The last message is from Lorraine. When I hear her voice, I hit the bottle again and listen close as she says, "Mark. This is it. If I ever see you again, I'll have no choice but to get a restraining order. This is for your own good." She hangs up, and I yank the cord from the machine and drag it behind me as I go from room to room, gathering every last trace of Lorraine into a black garbage bag.

I must be going through her stuff for a couple hours because it's already dark by the time Sam's headlights beam through the windows. I meet him at the door because I know he'll want to hear about everything that happened with Lorraine and how crazy she is for threatening to put a restraining order on me, but he starts with, "Why are you walking around the house in the dark again?"

I point to the empty bottle of whiskey where the answering machine once sat, then I point to the broken machine on the floor. He just nods and gives me a hug, patting my back.

I look him in the eye and say, "Hey, Sam, what do you say we go get a drink? Just us two, brothers, roommates, bros—"

"I can't tonight, Mark," he says. "I actually need to talk to you. I decided to move in with Sylvia."

I laugh because it was only a few months ago he was begging to come live with me since he couldn't stand living with our parents anymore. I told him he could stay as long as he wanted, rent free, until Lorraine was done with school and all moved in to her place. I guess none of that matters now.

"I was going to take some things over there tonight and stay," he says. "If that's all right."

"Sure, sure, sure," I say. "You can keep your stuff, or whatever, here as long as you need." I nod what feels like two hundred times.

"We can grab a drink later this week, though, okay?" He puts his hand on my shoulder. Sometimes, looking at my little brother is like looking in a mirror showing a reflection of the past me. We look similar enough, same hair color and style, same stature, same scruff. We both have dad's grey eyes and mom's firm chin. I see a familiar sparkle in his eyes. Mine used to shine like that, too. I know he loves Sylvia. He's been with her for years, and he thinks in his heart that this is the right thing to do, but I want Sam's eyes to never lose that sparkle.

"Sam, you've got to think about what you're doing," I warn him. "There is no pain greater than what the woman you love can bring you."

"I know, I know. I'll keep that in mind." I follow him up to his room. He packs clothes, bathroom supplies, and a stack of notebooks into his book bag.

"No, I'm not drunk. I'm telling you the truth." I have both my palms pressed together, sort of bowing to him like I'm Zen Master Seight.

"Look, Mark, I know you had your heart broken," he goes back down the stairs. I try to slide down the railing, but I fall on my ass. "But that doesn't necessarily mean I'm going to get my heart broken, too."

"You might think moving in with Sylvia is the right decision," I look up at him from the floor. "But what I'm trying to tell you is that if you love this girl, maybe you should wait. Maybe you should get married first."

"I appreciate you looking out for me. But Sylvia's not Lorraine, Mark."

I stretch out on the floor and try to keep from ripping my hair out. In the shards of the answering machine I see the little cassette tape lying there in perfect condition. I reach out for it and hold it an inch or so from my face. I open my mouth and bite down hard on it, but before I hurt my gums I see Sam looking at me, his eyebrows smashed together and his hands held up like I'm a feral dog.

"Sorry," I spit out the tape. "Look at me. This is what I've become. How do you do, it, Sam? You have it all figured out. You're happy. You're living the dream."

He sits down on the floor across from me.

"I just do what I do, and I follow my heart, and everything just feels right."

"That doesn't make any sense. I follow my heart, I do what feels right, and I don't even know who I am anymore."

"You're Mark Woodward. You're my big brother. You were born in Toledo, Ohio. Your sister is Zoe Woodward. She's a headache. Our parents are crazy, but they're impossible not to love. You went to the University of Toledo and studied business, and you turned out to be a hell of a businessman and you've got big dreams to expand your company. You were in love for six long years and you got dealt a bad card because the girl you love fell out of love and broke your heart to pieces, and even though you've been ripped apart, you're smart enough to know how to put yourself back together again."

Sometimes I wish my siblings and I all shared the same knowledge, but the fact is we all got a bunch of different pieces of the puzzle. In this instance, my little brother already has his corner of the puzzle all assembled, and I can't help but admire him for it.

"I don't know," I say. "Sometimes I don't know if I ever even wanted any of that, or if I just invented it all because I knew I was supposed to want something."

"The way I see it, you have to focus on the little things. You're always thinking about the big picture. Buying houses. Remodeling houses. What if you just try to think microscopically?"

I try to wind the tape back into the cassette. "Like what?"

"Like, when I'm not writing or with Sylvia, sometimes I like to reupholster furniture. I like to take the old, worn fabric and put a brand-new skin on it. Every time, you just have to pay attention and you just kind of get lost in it."

I ask him how I would go about reupholstering furniture, and he says he's got some leftover materials I could use. He starts in on this grim rust-orange chair he picked up off the street. He goes about cutting the old fabric and shedding its skin like a snake. He takes the skeleton in his hands as if cradling a child. As he glues new padding, I imagine it to be the muscles of the chair. I watch him wrapping the fresh hunter-green fabric around the padding and the frame. The last step is for him to sew it all together. He sews one side of the fabric, which is perfectly aligned and perpendicular, with the precision of a master craftsman. The rest of the chair he leaves exposed, in need of surgery.

"I've got to get going," he says. "Go ahead and finish it if you're feeling inspired."

I'm too tired to get him to stay or to try to make him see the whole moving in with Sylvia thing my way, and even though I know it's going to end badly with him in tears and breaking down, I know he'll just have to make those choices and figure everything out on his own, and all I can estimate is that some people are just meant to feel pain and others aren't. It's probably just as true that there's no point in thinking I have any say in Sam's destiny, or my own for that matter, so I wait a while after listening to his car pull out of the driveway before getting back up and turning all the lights on in the house and opening all the windows. The wind is piercing, fierce—but its howl is more comforting than the silence of this empty shell of a house.

I go to the garbage bag full of Lorraine's stuff and rifle through it one more time, caressing each item, saying goodbye to the memories, goodbye to Lorraine, and even though I want to douse the entirety of the contents in gasoline and turn it into a bonfire out in the back yard, I walk it out to the garbage bin, lug it inside, and close the lid. When I get back to the house, there's nothing. No Sam, no Zoe, no Claire or Ms. Engleson or Mr. Rayner, or veranda, or Muffy, or mattress, or bed frame, or Demetrius, or fire, or Lorraine, or retroactive thinking, or red motorcycle helmet with a distorted Mark Woodward trapped on it with no escape. I sit cross-legged on the ground across from the quarter-reupholstered chair. I see the clock strike three. I put a needle in my left hand, a thread in the right. I aim to meet them both at the eye, and make a promise to myself that I'll have something new by daylight.

The Al Capone Suite

*D*arryl got a job cleaning rooms and working the front desk at the Park Lane Radisson in downtown Toledo. It was her preference to work the night shift when the real creeps and crazies showed their faces, between midnight and sunrise. When Darryl interviewed for the job, her boss, Mr. Ornacki, a stout, balding man with a graying ponytail, bragged about all the stars that used to stay at Park Lane during its heyday.

"We've had our fair share of celebrities," the man said. "You name it. Miss Marilyn Monroe, herself. Ella Fitzgerald. Bob Hope. Cary Grant. And, my personal favorite—," he leaned across his desk, his voice at a whisper, "the notorious gangster Al Capone."

Darryl's eyes widened at the name, as if to impress her potential employer, even though she wasn't familiar with Al Capone's crimes.

"Are people allowed to stay in the room?" she asked. "Was there blood in it?"

The man's eyebrows wriggled like caterpillars.

"Some might say that is part of the allure of the suite." He opened the bottom drawer of his desk and lifted a key ring with his pinky. "Would you like the grand tour?"

⟨∘⟩

Once Darryl and Mr. Ornacki were inside the suite, Mr. Ornacki locked the dead bolt and cracked his knuckles. "Just our luck," he said. "The suite happens to be vacant. We can really take our time now."

"So, this is it?" Darryl said, inching further into the vintage-designed room. The walls, pale greens and blues, bounced light from the wide window overlooking the Maumee River. With the oceanic beams coming through, Darryl felt like she was in an aquarium, Mr. Ornacki an eel writhing around her.

"As you can see, we have retained the Modernist and Art Deco interior." He sat down on the velvet, celadon couch and stretched his hairy arm across its crest rail. "You happen to be standing in the very spot where Mr. Capone himself purchased the tommy gun he'd use in the Saint Valentine's Day Massacre from the then-owner of Park Lane."

Darryl looked down to her feet, imagining the transaction taking place—the dirty cash, the cold steel and bullet shells. She realized working at the hotel was her dream job.

"Are there many opportunities for growth in this establishment?" she said.

"I'm going to say to you what Al Capone said to the owner before he shot him on an earlier replica of this couch." Mr. Ornacki eyed Darryl up and down, circling his palm on the cushion beside him. "'Why don't you come over here and find out?'"

She sat down beside him, resisted the urge to shudder when his sweaty fingers pinched the back of her neck. As he mounted, her clothes found their way to the ornamental flowers woven into the Persian rug. Darryl would have liked to think that it wasn't the only thing that got her the job. This was the first time she'd been with a man since leaving Murfreesboro. She would have liked to admit that it wasn't going to happen again.

"I got a good feeling about you," Mr. Ornacki whispered in her ear, that familiar reek of booze on his breath. An image came to Darryl's mind—the Park Lane owner lying perforated with bullet holes, the baby-faced gangster standing over him. Life and death, she thought, her eyes focused on the rays of seafoam light. Shacking up wasn't exactly her top priority after her life fell apart and her siblings had to save her with a good old intervention. How could she possibly think of being with a man or having sex after her son's accident? Darryl switched to autopilot after the funeral, after leaving Florida, after returning to her isolation in Tennessee. It was a miracle she lasted the two months until her siblings drove down to her rescue.

Her older sister, LaShae, and their baby brother, Zane, abducted Darryl from her downtrodden house in Murfreesboro and transplanted her to Toledo. Three years, four jobs, and one suitor later and Darryl was no closer to escaping depression than she was in her overgrown hillside garden eating dead, rotted blueberries. At least in the thicket of wilted flowers and bruised, heart-shaped tomatoes, she wasn't chastised for reading Sylvia Browne instead of the Bible. Her siblings didn't know what it was like to wonder if every stray animal that walked into their yards could be the reincarnation of their child. They didn't know how loud darkness spoke, that spectral hymns were the only logic to its empty volume. Believing that the penumbral presence could be her son was the only thing that made Darryl's sleepless nights bearable.

She didn't argue with her siblings about leaving Tennessee for Ohio. Zane singlehandedly packed most of her entire house into the back of a U-Haul while LaShae kept Darryl from drowning in misery.

"That's the price we pay for loving with our whole hearts," LaShae said. "That's the cost of love."

"What exactly is the cost of love?" Darryl said, a bottle of rum clenched in her fist.

"The pain of loss," LaShae said. "The cost of love is the pain of loss."

"Like you know the pain of loss," Darryl said. Her bottle of rum was empty. Her heart felt the same way.

"We both lost our father, brother, and aunt in a car accident on Christmas Eve in 1972." LaShae's eyes locked on Darryl, her nose scrunched beneath indented, painted-on brows. "We were both forced to learn how to grieve when we were children. I can't have children, so no—I'll never be able to fully understand what you're going through. But I am your sister and I can tell you what I've learned. There's only one person you can love with your whole heart and never feel the pain of loss. Our Lord and Savior, Jesus Christ."

"And one thing I've learned," Darryl said, "is that there is no point in loving a god who lets your son take his life. Like I would want to be in heaven without my child."

Outside, Zane cursed as a box dumped to his feet, the result of Darryl's shoddy job at packing up her life. He lit a cigarette, kicked something metal, and slammed the door before walking inside to find his sisters in a heap on the floor.

"New plan," he said. "I'm not going to break my back trying to get all this into a truck. Take a day to get the things you absolutely need, and you can stay with me until you get on your feet."

⟨∞⟩

Three years and still Darryl wasn't on her feet, living in the spare room of her brother's house with barely any money in the bank. Since working at the hotel, Darryl paid for the groceries and even helped with Zane's electric bill. It was the least she could do to feel like she wasn't freeloading. A month into the job and Darryl already had the flow of Park Lane ingrained like second nature. For once she felt like there was hope in retaining a job, that she might actually be good at something. Looking down at Mr. Ornacki sprawled out on the celadon couch after their biweekly "security inspection," Darryl would button her jeans and think that she could do his job and then some.

Each night she learned as much as she could about the business and upkeep of the hotel. She was surprised at how many of the hotel guests were regulars, practically living out of the overpriced rooms. Half of her job entailed chasing away visitors that were unpaid for, louses trying to take advantage of the hotel's amenities for free. *No, sir. Not on my watch.* Darryl had been let go of on the spot plenty of times to know not to let this job slip through her fingers.

⟨∞⟩

One Saturday night, Park Lane was at maximum capacity due to a technology fair at the Convention Center. Darryl hadn't seen

Park Lane with no vacancy since the week she started and the president was in town. Every hour, she double-checked the registry to verify the number of guests that were allotted to each room. Next to the occupancy list she kept a notepad and tallied the different people who walked in and out of the doors: tired businesspeople, kicked-out husbands, potential prostitutes—these were the categories with the most tallies.

So far, the number of guests equaled since the start of her shift—not a single guest over the allotted count in the hotel registry. She was hoping that Mr. Ornacki would see how tight she could run a shift and promote her to assistant manager. Maybe then she'd be able to afford moving out of Zane's house.

It was quiet for a Saturday night, the only ruckus coming from Rochelle Evans, a robe-wearing elderly lady in room 205. Complaints rang though to Darryl's desk about a sound similar to a cat's yowling, in-heat mew. Darryl worried that Rochelle had snuck in secret suitors. Maybe she's just trying to get herself off, Darryl thought. Lord knew she'd been on that side of loneliness long ago—but she'd never let a hotel full of people hear her in the process.

Darryl picked up the desk phone and dialed room 205.

"Hello?" Rochelle said, voice drawn out like static.

"Hi, Rochelle, this is the front desk," Darryl said.

"Everything's fine, Darryl," Rochelle said, her heavy breaths metronome-constant.

Darryl fanned the pages of her book.

"Could you just keep it down, please?" Darryl asked. She flipped through the chapter about how to discover your own past life.

"What are you reading tonight?" Rochelle asked.

"Sylvia Browne," Darryl yawned. "*The Other Side and Back*."

"You know all that stuff is a sham, right?" The woman sounded amused. "It's all a bunch of new age hooey. Don't believe everything you read, Darryl."

"I'll take stock in whatever I'd like, thank you very much," Darryl said. "And we'd appreciate it if you kept your voice down, please. It sounds like there is a wild animal dying in your room. Thank you. Goodnight."

Darryl slammed the phone down and smiled. She wasn't about to let some town-maiden destroy the one thing that kept her connected to her son.

When 2:30 A.M. rolled around, Darryl made her rounds to each floor of the building for routine security inspection. Desk clerks were instructed to check four times throughout their shift to make sure there were no emergencies or alarming activity. Everything seemed fine until she got to the third and final floor. This was where the penthouses and most celebrity suites were, mostly reserved for VIP guests. Tonight Dr. MacMorton, a scientist, occupied the Al Capone suite. Darryl had helped him with a late check-in on the first night of the technology convention.

"Is there a bell boy?" Dr. MacMorton had asked. He'd peered down at her through his thick glasses and reddened, copper mustache. Darryl wasn't able to pinpoint his accent, though she guessed it was somewhat European. "Or perhaps a doorman? I need some help taking very fragile equipment to my suite."

"I'm the clerk, bell boy, door man, and maid," Darryl joked. The man didn't return a laugh. "I'd be happy to help you with your equipment."

The largest piece required a special dolly to wheel up to room 317. It was twice the size of the scientist, shaped like the Liberty Bell. The product looked unfinished, as if it needed a coat of paint or polished plastic. Wires stuck out through metal tubes and fine glass protruded, unprotected. While Darryl pulled the contraption behind her, the scientist kept a distance with his fingers extended, ready for something to fall apart.

Once inside the room, the scientist gathered the miscellaneous pieces, hoisted the machine from the dolly, and began reassembling it on the floor between the two double beds.

"You expecting company?" Darryl asked.

The scientist looked up from his tooling hands. "Oh, you mean the beds. It was all that was available on such short notice." His voice went hoarse as his gaze returned to the device. "And quite my luck to stay in the same room as Al Capone."

"Don't mean to be rude—it's just my job. Can't lose this one, too."

"A good vocation is difficult to acquire these days," Dr. Mac-Morton said, eyes fixed on connecting a monitor larger than the hotel television to the bell-shaped machine. "I understand Mr. Capone utilized the convenience of Toledo while expediting bootleg whiskey from Chicago to New York. As far as ethics are concerned within the perimeter of this facility, I'm sure you lean on the side of virtue."

He stuck out his hand to shake hers, a twenty rolled between his fingers.

"No tip necessary," Darryl said. "Just happy to do my job."

"Virtue," the scientist repeated. "An unlikely quality in such a fragile economy."

Now, standing outside of the Al Capone suite, Darryl stood in the glow that beamed from the crack between the scientist's door and the carpet. A muffled *zap* accompanied each flicker of the light. It reminded her of oversized beetles getting fried in her old electric bug trap.

It first occurred to Darryl that the light and sounds came from the television inside the room. She hovered in front of the door, body quarter-turned to walk the other way in case the door to room 317 suddenly flew ajar. The *zaps* grew less frequent, the light on the floor dimming to blackness.

Then came the sound of a moan—not the pleasurable kind coming from Rochelle Evans in 205, but the kind a person lets out when witnessing something both terrible and beautiful at the same time. The kind of moan her ex-husband let out when their first son, Christopher, was born. Not as unhinged as the kind of moan she let out when she got the call that their second son, Clark, had died.

"Hello?" a soft, sheepish voice called from the other side of the door.

Darryl froze where she stood. That doesn't sound like Dr. MacMorton, she thought. With the occupancy list in her hand, she reaffirmed that room 317 was checked out to only one guest.

Someone's in there who shouldn't be, she realized. It was her duty as night clerk to verify that no unaccounted guests occupied the rooms.

"Don't let my hotel become a whorehouse," Mr. Ornacki said on her first shift alone. "And keep an eye out for gangsters. Toledo ain't like Murfreesboro."

Now the entire corridor was silent and dark.

"Hello?" the bleating voice cried again. "Hello? Daddy?"

Darryl's head turned as she inched away from the door. Her fist floated in air, prepared to knock, though she couldn't will herself to disturb the muted air of the third floor. As she began to tiptoe away, the door flung open, filling the dark hallway with a pale verdant glow.

"Is there anything I can help you with?" the scientist said.

"I heard something," Darryl said. "Someone. Someone else."

The scientist cocked his head, the green light refracting from his round eyeglasses.

"You're a perceptive woman." He stood aside, allowing entry into the radiant suite. "I'm working on a very important project. For the convention. I'm afraid I'm quite behind in my work."

"Who is in there with you?" Darryl said.

"See for yourself, I am unattended." He nodded, urging for Darryl to enter. "The voice you heard was a projection from the machine you saw previously."

She stepped forward, feigning courage as the strange light enveloped her. The door closed behind her, the bolt locking automatically. She turned the corner past the bathroom and there it loomed—the machine, its fragments constructed into a towering hourglass-shaped monolith that stood from floor to ceiling.

A sculpture, she thought. A monstrosity.

"The voice you heard belonged to my daughter. She's no longer with us. Passed two years ago. She was seven."

Darryl felt her breath escape.

"It's not easy to bury your child," she said.

"No," Dr. MacMorton said.

I know how you feel, she wanted to say, to share in the connection of loss with the stranger. Instead she moved over to the machine where, upon a large computer monitor, there shone the image of a little girl's smiling face. One of her front teeth was missing.

"It's still in beta testing," the scientist said, "but the results have been surprisingly accurate. It's supposed to go live at the convention this week for the first time."

"I don't understand," Darryl said. "What is this? What does it do?"

"The idea is to utilize figments of data from people's lives and recreate a digital, interactive persona of an individual. I believe that it will be able to help those who have experienced great loss. Imagine being able to talk to a loved one after they are deceased. However, I've only been able to run the software with data coded from my daughter. And since her life was so short, the system doesn't have many facts or personality traits to work with."

"My youngest son was nineteen when he passed," she said.

The scientist removed his glasses and stepped closer to Darryl.

"Access to your son's belongings, anything that could recreate his digital persona—it could help me advance the demonstrative presentation at the convention."

Darryl wished she'd kept her mouth shut. There was a reason she never brought up her son's death in conversation.

"I'm not sure that would be a good idea. I don't know if I'm ready for something like that."

"Allow me to ask you a question. Have you ever lay awake at night, tossing, turning, questions rolling around the creaky floors of your mind like marbles? Questions you wish you could ask but will never have the chance to?"

Every night, Darryl wanted to say.

"I know I have," the scientist went on. "It's why I created this machine. I knew that I wouldn't be able to rest until I could see her face again, speak to her as if she were really here."

The machine overshadowed Darryl and the scientist. His daughter's toothless grin widened under blinking eyes.

"Isn't that right, Vanessa?" He reached up, stroked the monitor's frame with his hand.

"That's right, Daddy." Her rosy cheeks, round face, and pigtails reflected off each lens of the scientist's glasses.

⬯⬯⬯⬯

Instead of going to church Sunday morning with LaShae and Zane, Darryl searched the dank basement for the last traces of Clark—water-damaged boxes collecting mold and cobwebs. She couldn't get the image of Dr. MacMorton's machine out of her head. His daughter's voice sounded awfully real—organic, yet hollow. *Access to your son's belongings, anything that could recreate his digital persona*—the scientist's tone had gone from mournful to ambitious. Out of the five boxes Darryl brought from Tennessee, three of them contained the remnants of her son's life. Her siblings didn't question whether or not these objects would be a waste of space in the end, and now they might actually prove helpful in the name of science.

Once everything was stacked in a neat pile upstairs, Darryl fought the urge to plug in Clark's computer. After three cigarettes she decided that resisting was futile. She pushed the *ON* button of the laptop, hoping for the hundredth time to find answers to the questions that prevented her from sleeping. The old Dell computer beeped as it illuminated through the cracked screen. A photo of bright, sunny Tampa lay behind scattered files and folders on the desktop.

With her hand on the computer's mouse, Darryl stared, transfixed, at the photo of Tampa as if she were there again. Nineteen years had passed since she gave birth to Clark there, and twenty-two years since her first son, Christopher. She left Florida to escape her ex-husband eight years ago. Clark took his life there three years ago to the day. Darryl thought that the folders and files in disarray, scattered across the Tampa coastline, were a reflection of her son's mind. Little squares with indiscernible names overlapped each other, the natural system of rows and columns foregone in order to compensate his frantic, unorganized workflow.

The folder that she had been unable to open in the last year, the folder whose innards gave her relentless anxiety, was titled "Goodbye," and lay overlapping a photo icon of Clark's fiancée, Sasha. Darryl double-clicked "Goodbye," and the folder instantly widened to the size of the screen. A single file, an untitled text document, was saved inside the folder. A lightning-sharp migraine jolted through Darryl's temples. I should get some rum for this, she thought, but before she realized it the text document had opened and her eyes fixed on the opening words.

> *Dear mom,*
>
> *I am really scared because I keep thinking that I can't make her happy anymore. Maybe I'm not the right man for her. I keep thinking of suicide—*

Darryl heard Zane's truck pulling into the driveway. She coughed, her throat dry, lungs heaving, and shoved her thumb onto the laptop's power button. The front door opened before she could put a blanket over the open boxes of Clark's old things. She heard LaShae's voice, upbeat with post-church rigor.

"Pastor Luke had a good point when he brought up Peter 2:24—*he himself bore our sins.*"

"I think I might need to take a break from ushering," Zane answered. Darryl heard him go to the fridge for a beer.

"I take it I didn't miss anything new," Darryl said. She had appeased LaShae and went on Easter Sunday, but her visits had admittedly grown less frequent.

LaShae looked around at the boxes Darryl had dredged upstairs.

"Is everything okay?" she asked. "Should I call Pastor Luke?"

"It's not what you think," Darryl said. "At the hotel there's this man. A scientist. He built a machine that will let me talk to Clark."

LaShae sat down in the recliner next to Darryl and unfolded the wrapper of a stick of gum. "I don't think that machine will let you talk to Clark any more than Sylvia Browne will, Darryl." LaShae stuck the gum in her mouth, smacked her lips as she chewed.

In the kitchen Zane fumbled to secure his beer properly in its cozy. Outside, the sharp whistle from a train echoed—the tracks behind Zane's house were close enough to shake the small building when freighters passed. As the train grew closer, the siblings stayed silent, prepared for the deafening sound to drown each other out.

◇◇◇◇

Darryl packed the laptop, photographs, journals, letters, birthday cards, and voice messages into a duffel bag and kept it under the front desk for the entirety of her shift. Although tempted to fiddle with the contents of the bag, she kept her eyes on the guests passing through, often half-awake in walking comas. Whenever the lobby emptied, she'd reach for the duffel bag, stop herself, and instead reopen *The Other Side and Back*. What would Sylvia Browne say about the scientist's machine? Darryl could summon Sylvia's raspy smoker's voice from the countless audiobooks she'd borrowed from the Lucas County library. *We choose this life before we come to this body*, she envisioned Sylvia saying. *We each search for our own Truth.*

There was nothing saying that she had to go to room 317 after her shift. She could call the suite and tell Dr. MacMorton that she'd changed her mind, that she didn't like the thought of her son's afterlife as a science experiment.

The front desk phone chimed and Darryl dropped *The Other Side and Back* to the floor.

"Front desk," Darryl answered.

"Is there something wrong, Darryl?" It was Rochelle Evans from room 205, her breaths slow and distanced for once. "You haven't called to check in tonight. And I didn't see you walking the halls. I was worried about you."

"What do you think happens to our souls?" Darryl said. Sylvia Browne's photograph stared at her from the floor next to Clark's duffel bag.

"I once heard that Native Americans refused to have their photographs taken," Rochelle said. "They thought it would steal their soul. Disrespected the spirit world. But what do I know about the soul? I can't even keep a man."

"Everything is fine," Darryl said before hanging up. "And thank you for checking." As she clicked the phone to the receiver, she looked up to find Mr. Ornacki standing over her with *The Other Side and Back* in his hands.

"I told you about reading on the job," he said. "How can I expect you to keep my hotel under control if you're busy reading this hocus pocus crap?" He dropped the book into the wastebasket and shook his head.

"I guess there's probably not much room for growth here, then," Darryl said. She picked up the duffel bag and started around the desk. "And to think I wanted to be assistant manager."

"Right," Mr. Ornacki said, cracking a yellow-toothed grin. "You'd have to put out a lot more to move up in a place like this, honey."

"You can find yourself a new clerk," Darryl said. She reached into the garbage can, withdrew the now coffee-stained copy of *The Other Side and Back*. "I ain't your damn whore."

༄

The scientist waited for Darryl and opened the door as soon as he saw her through the peephole.

"I thought you might not show," he said. He took the bag from her hands and searched its contents while Darryl lingered in the corridor.

"I brought what you asked for," she said.

He took the duffel bag from her hands, surprised by its weight.

"I do believe this will suffice," he said.

Darryl followed him into the suite. The same glow, like nuclear energy, radiated from the monitor attached to the towering machine. Dr. MacMorton splayed the contents of the duffel onto the corner-most bed. Clark's laptop. Photographs. Journals. Letters. Birthday cards. Voice message tapes. Darryl grimaced as the scientist ran his gloved fingers along the items.

"Be careful with all that, please," Darryl said. "I don't have anything backed up. It's all I have left of him."

"Don't you worry," the scientist said. "I treat all of my test subjects with the utmost care and tenderness. I'll need to do some troubleshooting with the equipment before we get started."

"Do you mind if I sit down, then?" she asked.

"Of course not. Please, please," Dr. MacMorton motioned to a chair and opened Clark's laptop. "First I'll have to access all of his social profiles, emails, messages, photos, archives—you know, the basic data that guides behavioral information."

"Right," she said. "Behavioral information."

His fingers clacked on the keyboard the way Clark's once did. Would his fingerprints be erased after this? After forty minutes of tinkering with the laptop Dr. MacMorton alternated to the photographs and scanned them all, one after the other popping up on the monitor attached to the bell-shaped machine.

"Now to copy vocal patterns," said the scientist. He inserted the voice message tapes into an old-fashioned player, updated to connect with the monitor.

"Hey, mom, it's just me," a voice rang from the monitor's speakers.

Darryl sprang back, nearly tipping the chair over.

"Wanted to call and tell you Happy Birthday." The voice was youthful, male with a slight Southern drawl.

"I wasn't expecting to hear that," Darryl said.

"My apologies," the scientist said. "If you'd prefer, I can mute the voice messages until we begin the test run."

"Yes, I would prefer," Darryl said.

"Right, then." The scientist continued troubleshooting without another word to Darryl. Watching him pick through Clark's things gave her chills, as if witnessing a coroner at work on a corpse, the suite his makeshift mortuary. After an hour, he turned to her and said, "It is still an imperfect product." Darryl blinked, double-taking the image of her son's face on the monitor. It smiled when it saw her, glitching with every small movement. "We put more emphasis on the reliability of the intelligence. We will smooth out the presentation once we receive more funding."

Darryl felt a dampness envelop her skin. The air in the hotel room went cold. From inside the machine came a sound like a flock of hummingbirds flapping their miniscule wings. The motor, Darryl thought. Don't forget that this thing is just a machine.

"Hey, Mom," spoke the image of Clark on the monitor. His brown eyes, his wide grin—it was not so different than Skyping with Christopher. The picture lagged and then resumed Clark's natural flow of movement.

Darryl looked to the scientist. "It's perfectly normal to respond to it," he said. "It can recognize you and operates with full retina registration. It sees your movement; it hears you speak."

Clark's face retained its smile, waiting for Darryl to answer. If only she were really Skyping with him. If only it were really her son greeting her so casually.

"Hi, Clark," she said. The inside of her stomach heaved. She wanted to suck the words back into her forever. She wondered if machines knew the difference between ghosts and angels.

"How are you?" the image asked. "How is everything? How's Chris?"

Darryl looked to the scientist, unable to keep her eyes on the monitor. It felt like looking at the sun—if she stared for too long, she'd go blind.

"What is the point of this?" she said. "Why would I tell all my personal information to a computer? It doesn't care about Chris."

"He might," the scientist said. "It's a symbiotic experience, this technology. It possesses a type of intelligence similar to playing chess against your computer—only on a much larger, powerful, personal scale."

"That machine is not my son," she said.

"Of course not. This machine lacks a soul. But if you approach the machine with an open mind, you may discover uncanny resemblances between its ability to relay information and your son's unique, individual personality."

A series of thuds came from the other side of the door—even Clark's digital eyes averted to seek out the cause of the noise. "You got my woman in there?" a groggy voice said. It was Mr. Ornacki's—drunk, Darryl estimated. "You in there, Darryl? You think you can just quit and sleep around with my guests?"

"This was a bad idea," Darryl said. She reached for the illuminated buttons on the machine, pressing randomly in hope of making Clark's face disappear.

"Stop it," the scientist said. "You could damage my work—you could ruin everything."

"I'll break this damn door down, you hear?" Another series of thuds came from Mr. Ornacki.

"Dear Mom," Clark's voice started. "I am really scared because I keep thinking that I can't make her happy anymore."

"Turn it off," Darryl cried.

"I keep thinking of suicide," Clark went on.

"The system must be erratically accessing data from the hard drive," Dr. MacMorton said, his attention on the needs of the machine.

"I don't care what it's accessing," she said. "Turn it the hell off!" She started to gather Clark's assorted belongings from the hotel bed, shoving them back into the duffel.

"I just wanted to love her, mom, but she didn't love me back," Clark's voice started to break up, like the other end of a long-distance call. "I'm sorry, Mom. I just wanted her to love me back."

The suite's door flew open with a booming crack, the sound like a sharp axe to fresh timber. Mr. Ornacki stood in the doorframe, his shadowed silhouette rising and falling with each breath.

"I don't understand," the scientist said. "I pulled the power. The system should be down; the machine should not be running."

"Please forgive me," said Clark's face on the monitor. "I just couldn't see another way to not feel like this."

"It's okay," she said. All the lights in the suite went out except for her son's face, its glow combating the darkness. She ran to the monitor and cradled it in her hands. "Everything's going to be okay. Momma loves you."

Andie Comes Home

She returned to Toledo after four years with a broken heart and a U-Haul full of things she didn't need. Neal had left her for another woman after six years together, and to top it off, he'd eloped with the woman before Andie even had a chance to leave Los Angeles.

"Maybe you can get a job with the film commission in Columbus," her father said. He limped while carrying her box of clothes from the U-Haul to the front door of the house she grew up in.

Home for less than ten minutes, Andie thought, and I already feel like I'm being kicked out. The April sun felt cooler on Andie's skin than she remembered, but it was better than the snowstorms in Colorado and tornadoes in Utah.

The screen door swung open and out ran a little girl with curly brown hair.

"Sissy!" the girl cried. She ran straight from the door to Andie's open arms.

"Hi, bummy," Andie said. She hoisted her sister into the air and kissed her from cheek to cheek.

"Where's Neal?" the girl asked.

Andie's smile fell flat.

"Amy, we talked about this, remember?" Their father struggled to open the screen door with the box of clothes in his hands. "We don't talk about Neal around Andie, right?"

"I know, dad," Amy snapped. "I'm sorry, Andie." The girl's eyebrows caved inward while a furled frown contorted upon her face.

"Don't be sorry, bum. It's okay." Andie forced a smile. The thought of Neal made her want to lock herself in her bedroom for days.

"Poke you in the dimples," Amy said. The girl swabbed her tiny index finger into Andie's cheek. Her own smile stretched, absent of one front tooth.

Their mother flung open the screen door. Their father was knocked off his feet, spilling the box of clothes all over the front lawn.

"Nana Dotty's in the hospital," their mother said. She heaved, her face flush. "She had an accident. The doctor doesn't know if she's going to make it."

On the way to the hospital Andie sat in the backseat with Amy. She played with her sister's mermaid dolls the way Neal had done when they waited in line at Disneyland the past October.

"It's not the same as when we were stuck in Neverland," Amy said. Andie thought it a miracle that her sister's face wasn't soaked with tears. Things with Neal had seemed perfect then.

"What did we say, Amy?" their father asked from the passenger seat.

"We don't talk about Neal…" The pink mermaid in Amy's hand dove to the dirty floor of the car. Nobody spoke for the rest of the ride to the hospital.

When their mother parked the car in the hospital garage, she looked back to the girls, her eyes magnified by her thick glasses. "Just wait here while we talk to Nana," she said. "Give me about ten minutes with my mother and then bring Amy inside."

"Okay, Mom," Andie answered. She retrieved the lost mermaid from the ground and transitioned into playing.

"Where is Mommy going?" Amy asked. The tone in the girl's voice turned toward a whimper.

"No crying, okay?" Andie said.

"Okay." Amy embraced the pink doll with both hands and pressed it to her face.

The sisters sat quietly until Andie's phone buzzed. It was a text from Neal.

I'm sorry, the text read. Did you get home okay?

Andie looked at the time and, seeing that fifteen minutes had passed, she ignored Neal's text. Before helping Amy out of the car seat, she deleted Neal's number from her phone, even though she had it committed to memory.

Andie held Amy's small hand as they searched for Nana Dotty's room number in the Flower Hospital hallway.

"Wait!" Amy cried. The girl stopped in her tracks. "Shouldn't we go to the store and get something nice for Nana? Maybe some pretty, pink flowers."

"Maybe later, bum." Andie tugged gently at her little sister's hand.

"Please?" Amy's eyes puffed up, forming tears.

"Nana's waiting for us, Amy."

"I wish Neal was here."

Now Andie's eyes mirrored Amy's.

"Me, too."

"Is Nana Dotty going to die?"

Andie knelt down to her sister.

"Remember," Amy said. "No crying."

Andie cracked a smile and shed a single droplet that inked down her cheek. Amy poked her finger into one of Andie's deep dimples.

"Don't forget to smile," the girl said. She stepped forward and pulled Andie along. While Amy marched forward, Andie noticed that she did not read the room numbers as she passed them—she kept peering her head into each room until she saw their grandmother.

My moral compass is inferior to that of my five-year-old sister, Andie thought. She tried to force the thought of Neal out of her mind. With her free hand grasping her cell phone, Andie fought the urge to text him, but she couldn't resist typing his number from memory.

"Nana!" Amy released Andie's hand and rushed into their grandmother's room. Andie put the phone into her pocket before finishing Neal's number.

"Oh, hello, sweethearts," Nana Dotty said. The woman sat upright in her hospital bed, her face as pale as the walls of the room.

Andie's mother wept. Her wails echoed into the hallway.

"Nana, you can have my mermaid. We didn't get flowers." Amy held the doll up for her grandmother.

"Let's go," their mother said. "Nana wants to talk to Andie alone."

⚬⚬⚬

"There were men I loved before I married Papa," Nana told Andie. The two women held hands. "Some of them broke my heart, and I guess I broke some of theirs." Nana Dotty breathed with deep, wheezing gasps. "But in this life, you've got to make decisions. And you've got to live with the decisions you make, Andie. You can't go back."

Her grandmother's thin skin felt dry against hers. Andie rubbed her thumb across the top of Nana Dotty's wrinkled hand, and the room went silent.

Right Now at This Very Moment

As the snow fell and covered the highway roads leading to and away from the Knights Inn of Rossford, Ohio, Athen sat at the edge of his hotel bed, hand-rolling another cigarette, waiting for Sylvia Pryor—the last person on Earth with whom he ought to be trapped in a hotel room— to re-emerge from the steaming bathroom wearing nothing but her Guia La Bruna undergarments. He pursed the unlit cigarette between his lips and clicked the dial on the nightstand radio just as the voice on the other end announced the level three winter emergency approaching Northwest Ohio. It was impossible for Athen to escape the thought of what would be happening in the parallel universe where his best friend and Sylvia's sweetheart, Sam, hadn't been killed by a drunk driver on the shoulder of the Columbiana County Interstate, last July.

Sylvia's bottle of prescription Vicodin sat half-filled atop the nightstand, a baggy of marijuana resting in the upper half of it. They were out of vodka and it was only a quarter past midnight. It took Athen the next fifteen minutes to finish his cigarette when, finally, as the steam rolled out from under the bathroom door, he caught her in his crosshairs. Like a camera, he panned from her aubergine toenails to her gunmetal blue eyes. She leaned her hips against the doorframe, cracked a smile, and stood there with nothing to hide. Every ounce of morality within him screamed to look away, to be a gentleman. But he knew very well that she needed tonight as much as he did, because tonight could be an island. Tonight, they could go nowhere.

⁊⁊⁊⁊⁊

According to the calendar it had been six months since the accident, although for Athen and Sylvia it felt like all of history had collapsed on them and started anew. The accident, the funeral, the nine weeks in the hospital, the absence of a tombstone, the liquor and pills, the sleepless nights, the series of near overdoses; all of it may as well have never happened, or taken place centuries ago, in a separate lifetime. With Sam gone, they found in each other a way to fill the void his death created. When she was in Flower Hospital, and they waited for her recovery to tell her Sam was gone, Athen had been the one at her side. He was the one who, against her parents' wishes, wheeled her to the Urbanski Funeral Home to say goodbye. He was the one to answer her calls in the middle of the night. He was the one who would lie for hours in darkness with the phone to his ear, just breathing, because it was all he could do to help keep her sane. And in the eclipse of her agony, he was the one to help her remove the bandages and the engagement ring so that she could bear the small steps toward beginning again.

Athen had never intended to fall in love with Sylvia. Sam had been Athen's best friend since kindergarten. They considered each other brothers. When Sam started dating Sylvia during freshman year, she became a sister to Athen by association. With

Sam gone, it felt like a sin to have eyes for the girl he'd loved. Athen often recalled Sam telling him that he'd wanted to marry Sylvia, and the many ways he wanted to propose. All it took was one too many Whiskey-Sevens and a poorly installed catalytic converter to forge Athen and Sylvia together, despite their fever-ish guilt, alone in a hotel room for the first time with romantic intentions. Six months after the accident, and it seemed that Syl-via was finally ready to shovel dirt over the past.

Magnetism drew her away from the doorframe toward the edge of the bed where Athen sat, his heart racing and the last of the smoke drifting from his mouth. The sway of her body struck him as a tigress gliding through the brush toward its prey. She sat next to him, took the baggy of marijuana, and rolled a joint for them to share. Lying shoulder to shoulder, they passed it back and forth, exhaling thick clouds, noting how the stain on the ceiling resembled the Milky Way. As the smoke filled her lungs and her heart rate tripled, she was no longer afraid to lace her fingers with his, lean over him, and exhale softly.

The distance between their lips seemed to linger infinitely until, at last, the collision was irrevocable. Athen took what seemed an eternity to place his hand where Sylvia's jaw met her neck. He held his eyes shut for fear of the regret that would sink in when they opened. This moment was all he had before it could no longer be blamed on the pills or vodka. Even though it was Sylvia who invited Athen to the hotel to get away for the holiday, even though they had spent many nights wrapped in each other's arms, never had they flirted with their platonic affair becoming physical. Now the bridge had been crossed. Athen wondered if they could stand to live with what came next, whether a kiss would traverse or amplify the chasm between them.

Sylvia pulled back and gazed into Athen's eyes, her own drowned in pools of mascara.

"I'm sorry," she said before kissing him again, contradicting herself. Her teeth dug into his lower lip at a rhythm with her palm tightening around his.

She held him for a beat longer than last time and, unfastening the top button of his collared shirt, tore away from him to say, "I just can't do this." She rested her face against his chest, rising and falling with each breath. Athen wanted to tell her he loved her. But she stood and retreated back to the bathroom, the print of her mascara on his white shirt like a child's rendition of a ghost, and the prescription bottle disappeared from the nightstand.

⚬⚬⚬

This was not the first time Athen would have to charm Sylvia out of a locked bathroom; their relationship had been built on conversations had from opposite sides of them. He sat with his back to the door, listening to the bathwater Sylvia ran for the mere sake of its soothing sound. Bathrooms had become her haven, like an oratory at church where she could confess her most intimate stories of Sam. She could retrace the memories that were not quite memories, but images of events that had almost come to pass, or may have come to pass if only she had said this differently or done that earlier. She could scream, pound her fists on the door, or drink her weight in vodka; no matter what she did on the other side of the door, Athen made an unspoken promise to always be there, to always protect her. He owed that much to Sam.

With his eyes focused on the glowing digits of the alarm clock, he tried to gauge how many pills were left in that bottle, and how much time he had before she would be too far gone. It had been twenty minutes since he had heard anything but running water. He wanted to break the door open, press her against the cold tile floor and kiss her from the deepest part of him. He waited for a sign, knowing it would be too much too soon. Instead, he turned his face flush against the door and, out of key, began singing the Rolling Stones' "Beast of Burden."

The song was Athen's only call to arms. It was his way of letting her know that yes, he was concerned if she was still intact, if she was still holding it together. She sang along with him, tapped her knuckles against the door to the beat. It was just when they arrived at the repetition of "pretty girl" that the power went off in their room. It felt like just the sign Athen was looking for.

The faucet squeaked off, and she opened the bathroom door to collapse in his arms. In the hotel's darkness they entwined under the doorframe, half in the bathroom, half in the entryway. Once his eyes adjusted, he was able to look into hers. He checked the dilation of her pupils. Soon the pills would be in full effect. When she buried her head in his chest, he closed his eyes and breathed in the sweet scent of her hair, sugarplum, and caressed his palm along her shoulder blade, up to her neck. With each caress she let out a soft moan, and nudged his chin with her forehead like a kitten seeking affection.

Their solace was then interrupted by a knocking at the door. Sylvia didn't hesitate for a second to answer, wearing nothing but her undergarments. The hotel attendant at the door was as shocked as Athen to see her standing there, even in near-total darkness, with the door wide open.

"Ma'am," he said, "We are passing out candles for your inconvenience. We hope the power will return shortly."

"Can we have two, please?" she said. "This room really calls for two candles, don't you think?"

"Well, yes, ma'am. I suppose."

"You're a good man," she said to the attendant. "You've always been such a good man."

Then, after shutting the door in his face, she returned to the center of the room, lit both candles, and, taking a swig from the empty bottle of vodka, stood on the table between the candles. They cast an orange glow over her thighs. Athen, breathing heavily now more than ever, wanted to take her in his arms. But her show was just beginning. She flipped her hair across her face, hips swaying, and slowly kicked her legs while singing the rest of "Beast of Burden" in her sexiest voice.

But she couldn't quite finish the song. The lyrics trailed off, her mumbles proof that the Vicodin had kicked in. Worried she would fall from the table, Athen held out his hand like a gentleman, presenting her the option to climb down. Once her feet hit the ground, she folded into the dead center of him. He held her limp body up in a one-sided slow dance, whispering the remaining lyrics into her ear.

He pressed his lips to her forehead and breathed deep to hold the tears back. He rocked her back and forth in the silent room, as if there were music actually playing.

Her breath against his neck was finite, delicate. He opened his mouth to say, without hesitation, "It should have been me in that car. You don't deserve what you got. You're so damn good and you got the worst of it. Don't run away. Just be strong and one day it will all be okay."

She pried her eyes open just wide enough for him to see her vacuous pupils. With what seemed like all her strength, she put her fingertips to his cheek and said, "Don't stop, Sam. Don't you ever stop."

Hearing Sam's name took the air out of Athen. Even though he knew how gone she was, he wanted it to be real. He wanted it to be him. It was obvious, then, that he had two choices: He could keep his mouth shut, hold her firmly, slide her to bed, watch over her as she fell asleep, sit next to her, ride out the storm and, come morning, pretend as though nothing had happened. Or, aware of the fact that there would be no turning back, he could dig deeper. For just a little while longer, he could be Sam.

"I'll never stop," he said.

"Oh, Sam," she said. "It's always been you. Remember when we watched *Last Year at Marienbad*? I wanted to kiss you so badly."

"I wanted to kiss you, too."

"I'm sorry, Sam. I'm sorry about it all."

"Sorry about what, Sylvia?"

"About all of it," she said. "Every last bit of it."

Tears dripped from her eyes. She repeated, "Sam. Oh, Sam."

"Please tell me why you're sorry."

Between heaves she managed to say, "For the trip. And making you drive. And I never said goodbye. I never said goodbye because I didn't know. How could I know?"

The truth made Athen's throat tighten. Even though she needed him as a friend now, even though she needed him to relieve her guilt, he couldn't resist letting out what he thought he felt, and what Sam surely would have said.

"You couldn't have known, Sylvia. I know that. Don't be sorry, Sylvia. I love you, Sylvia."

"Always and forever, Sam?"

"Always and forever."

And as he stared down at her, he reeled in to kiss her, and he never took his eyes from hers. She opened them, slowly, and before their lips could touch again, she became aware of everything she had said, as if Athen were Sam, and Athen responding to her with conviction. Weak as she was, she pushed away from him and backed toward the door.

"Sylvia, please," he said, trying to keep her there. "It's not what you think."

"You don't care about this, Athen. You don't care about me. Or Sam. Or any of it. You're a damn liar. You're a goddamn liar." She opened the door and ran into the dark hallway. He chased her but she was already running toward the door that led to the parking lot. Calling her name didn't stop her from escaping, in her undergarments, past the red exit sign.

Passing the doorway, he looked around but could only see sections of the parking lot illuminated by streetlights, snow seeming to hover. Knowing anything about Sylvia's love for theatrics, Athen expected to find her in a mound of snow, holding her breath, openly praying aloud for death. But to his surprise, there she was, flat on her back and only a few feet away, fanning her arms and legs to make a snow angel.

"After half a bottle of Vicodin you really can't feel a thing," she said.

"That's not funny," he said. "Get up or you'll hurt yourself."

"Who's gonna make me? You and what army?" She made herself laugh loud and it echoed across the lot. He dug his arms between her skin and the pavement, lifted her up, and made his way back through the exit door.

Back in the hotel room, Athen set Sylvia down in the bathtub before gathering the bedding off the queen-sized mattress. He returned with the sheets and comforter, spread them over Sylvia, and climbed in next to her.

"You're wrong, you know," he said. "I do care about this. I do care about you. And no, I may not know what to make of it, but I'm here. I'm not going anywhere."

"You can't say that," she said. "You can't say you're not going anywhere and mean it, because how can you know? There is no way to know, so if you say that you're not going anywhere it's a lie. One minute you're here and the next minute you could be gone. The only thing you can know is what's here, right now, at this very moment, and all the things that got us here."

She paused.

"All the things that got us here," she repeated. "If my dad had never made me get a job at the zoo, I wouldn't have met Sam."

"If my parents had never moved into the house on Erie Street when I was five, I wouldn't have met Sam," Athen said. "It all goes back so far. Our friends, our parents. All of their reasons and desires and choices put together. And we're the sum of it all."

"And if Joel Marrington never stopped at the bar where he drank too much alcohol, he wouldn't have been trying to beat traffic by swerving into that shoulder lane," she said.

"Don't do that, Sylvia. Don't go there."

"And if I had never done that stupid play, and if Sam had never auditioned to impress me, we wouldn't have been broken down in the shoulder lane. And maybe if I was the one driving…"

"Sweetheart," he said.

"I'm sorry," she said. "But doesn't it feel like we're meant to be here? Just think of all the things that were put in place in order for us to be living in this moment. There is no moment in history like this moment. And we're alive in it together."

"There is nothing else in the world I would ask for."

Beneath the acrylic hotel blankets, cradled together in the bathtub, Athen and Sylvia lingered until morning, not saying another word. Hours passed before they fell asleep, and when the sunlight came, they hid from the day by retreating further under the blankets, still in each other's arms.

The Naga Dreams

*F*lames lick the walls of the rundown, vacant building. I search from one hollow room to the next, evading whipping lashes of crimson spittle. Upon discovering total emptiness in each room, unsure of what I'm searching for, I retreat back to the endless corridor that grows longer with every failed excavation. Cobbled stone litters the walkway, blocking my path to the stairwell leading to the roof.

When I extend my hand to create a path through the debris, I am not consumed by heat. My flesh is not seared. Rather, a surge of understanding rushes from my fingers to my heart. An understanding of what I'm searching for. Whom I'm searching for.

He is somewhere in this building. His face echoes in the chambers of my mind. I feel him, his presence, his energy, though in the enclave of the burning building his absence rages hotter than the wisps of cinder at my back.

I piece together the contours of his face, fragments of a shattered image. The harder I try to conjure his visage, the more the fractured shards of him slip away into the flames. Smoke curls in flumes with every parcel of him fed to blaze.

Is he waiting for me on the roof? An utterance rises through me—a combination of impulses that are reduced to symbols by the words that give them shape:

Seek.

Hunt.

Love.

Somewhere between the galvanized slate of roof and vermillion cloak of sky he waits for me—longs for one last kiss in the fire.

⟨≈⟩

I woke in a cold sweat, my linens soaked through, the image of fire still clear in my mind. The gray light of morning entered my bedroom like a weak fog. In the split second between dreaming and waking, I mistook the light to be smoke and choked from the dryness of my throat. I was alive. Awake. Alone. I extended my arm to see if the man from the dream lay next to me in my empty bed. The essence of the man lingered inside of me, something vivid about his abstract face. I could have wished all of the separate parts of his body into existence and assembled him myself.

Did I know the man? I rested my head back down onto the wet pillow and stared at the ceiling, allowing my body and nerves to discover peace again. I started to fall back into a trance, the gleams of light like spider webs stretching across the walls of my room. Almost entering another dream state, I was pulled to consciousness by the phone ringing.

"Hello?"

"Are you alright?" The voice quivered with panic. Raspy, male.

"Who is this?"

"It's Hollow. Are you alright? Are you safe?"

I hadn't heard from Hollow since his last film. When we wrapped, he'd pulled me aside behind the gamma tanks backstage where nobody could see or hear us.

"You brought so much life to this film," he'd said.

"Thank you."

"I've watched you go as an actress. As a dreamer."

"I couldn't have done it without you," I'd said.

"I want to leave my wife for you," he'd said.

"Virginia?" his voice escalated an octave. "Are you there?"

"I'm fine," I said. "What's going on?"

"The fire," he said. "I heard about the fire near the Valley. I wanted to make sure you were okay." I dialed in to the news broadcast and there it was, a blanket of orange engulfing the hills of Van Nuys. "Are you at home? They're telling everyone to evacuate." I got out of bed and looked out my window to find, not eighty yards away, reams of smoke barreling toward the sky.

"Yes, I'm at home. Where should I go? What should I do?" I ran to my closet and unhooked handfuls of clothes, threw them onto the bed. Realized clothes wouldn't help me escape the fire.

"Stay calm," Hollow said. "Remember that this is not a dream. Take note of all your sensory experiences."

"I don't need acting tips right now," I said. I was blasting water from my sink, trying to scoop it into Tupperware with cupped hands.

"It's called *Wildfire*," he said. "The name of my next picture. It's a romance. But it's fucked, Virginia. It's mental."

What was I going to do with a dozen plastic bins of water strewn about my apartment? I could smell singed earth filtering through the walls.

"I don't know if I'm ready for another movie right now, Hollow. I still don't feel the same since *Young Intrepid.*"

"You still having the nightmares?"

"Every night."

"Maybe we can decrease the gamma frequency this time around," he said. "This role should be a more natural fit for you."

Sirens bellowed outside my building. People calling from megaphones urged us to leave the building at once.

I said, "What about your wife?"

Fire trucks wailed stories beneath me. Hollow breathed heavily on the other end.

"We split," he said. "I thought you knew."

"Is this real?" I wanted to cry tears that could extinguish the flames outside.

"I'll email the script to you," he said. "You can read it on the train. We're shooting in San Francisco. See you in two days."

I didn't have a chance to respond. I didn't need to. Even though Hollow spoke for me, he wasn't wrong. He knew I couldn't turn down a role, or another chance to be with him.

"This is your last chance," the voice from the megaphone warned. "All residents *must* evacuate. The premises are not safe."

I stuffed the scattered clothes on the bed into a duffel bag along with a month's supply of medication to counter-act the gamma. With the orchestra of sirens outside, I couldn't think to pack anything else I'd need. Such is the life of an actor. Once it was time to inhabit this new character, I wouldn't need much else of Virginia, anyway.

⟳∞∞⟲

Wood and cloth beneath my feet. The lovers in the oil painting are forever separated. Smeared cerulean and red in layers on the tips of my broken fingers.

The naked man in the painting, the artist, stands next to me. His lover's breasts sag, gazing into me like tear-filled eyes. I've ruined her—us.

Now the me from his painting rises from the rubble of art, her oil-based flesh as flammable as my paper lips.

No kiss could surrender such an imperfect me.

With a can of varnish, I preserve their love and apply pungent thinner to my body.

❧

I opened my eyes on the train to find a young woman trying to hide the fact that she was staring at me. She sat across from me, her gaze shifting from me to the ocean outside our shared window. I shut my eyes again, hoping to signal that I wasn't in the mood for talking. But in the darkness of my mind I saw the artist from my dream again.

The painter had been Hollow. There was no denying it. I thought back to the reality of the dream, and in the dream it wasn't Hollow. At least not the way I knew him. There was no mistaking his appearance, though. He was and yet he was not Hollow.

I wondered if Hollow had ever said anything before about painting.

"I don't mean to bother you," the woman finally said, "but you're Virginia Wallace, aren't you? The actress? I saw you in *Young Intrepid*, and I thought you were phenomenal."

"Thank you," I said, keeping my eyes closed. "That was a tough role for me."

"I can only imagine. It's really something, isn't it? The way they make movies nowadays. You actors must have to learn so much about the way the brain works. To control your dreams like that. And the fact that they can *record* all the things you're thinking while you're asleep. It still blows my mind."

"It's really something," I said. I opened my eyes, smiled at the woman, and turned toward the ocean. There wouldn't be getting any more sleep with her across from me.

"Is it true what they say about what happened behind the scenes on *Young Intrepid*?"

I exhaled, slow and weary.

"I'm not sure what you're talking about," I lied.

She leaned forward on her seat, brought her voice to a whisper.

"About you and the director," she said. "They say that you two had a thing. That the movie was really about your secret flame."

The tabloids had had a field day with a photograph taken of Hollow and me in a dive karaoke bar one night after filming. I'd just finished a botched rendition of "Superstition." When I returned to my seat, Hollow and two shots of Cuervo Gold waited for me. He knew tequila was the only thing capable of making me kiss a married man in public. That's when I had started to need a boost in my gamma frequency during filming. The stress of Hollow's wife finding out about us prevented me from inducing the lucid dream on my own. Without focus I couldn't control a thing, my mind running amok with the guilt I'd felt from ruining Hollow's marriage.

"Don't believe everything you read in the papers," I said to the young woman.

ᠬᠣᠣᠣ

In the two days it took to get to San Francisco I had committed most of my lines to memory. In the film I was to play Amber Hardley, a zoologist who traverses the desert and a remote island searching for a legendary, prehistoric serpent once worshipped by indigenous cultures as a god. Amber fell in love, of course, with a daring archaeologist. The zoologist and the archaeologist needed each other to escape the island alive. Both of them nearly died when the serpent revealed itself to have abnormal intelligence and set fire to the island in order to trap the lovers.

From the train station I took a cab to the filming facility, wearing my sunglasses like a mask despite the hazy, stone-colored San Francisco sky. The sunglasses didn't prevent the driver from noticing who I was and turning to talk at every red light.

"You were really something in that movie about the astronauts who can't make it back to Earth."

"Thank you. That was a tough role for me."

"I can't believe you guys dream that stuff up," he said. "Me and the wife tried joint dreaming once. When we woke up and watched the recording it was all these jumbled, freaky images. Like bad reception on TV, or scrambled porn before there were cell phones."

He laughed, checking my reaction in his rear view.

I didn't speak. I wanted him to leave me alone. I needed to clear my mind and think about what I'd need to say when I saw Hollow, the perfect dialogue that would make him mine.

"Sorry, ma'am. Didn't mean no offense."

We both kept quiet until he pulled up to the road outside the gate surrounding the two-story stone building. I could hear the ocean slapping the side of the cliff behind the facility, particles of salt drifting in the air that wafted into my mouth when I breathed. The driver offered to help with my bags, but I declined. He pulled away, dirt spewing from beneath his tires. I picked up my bags and lugged them up the steps to the arching door.

The lobby walls were lined with posters of award-winning films created on site. *Traveling Alone*, *The Runaway Mistress*, *Under a Tourmaline Sky*. I wanted to be a part of a movie that mattered. I wanted to make art. I only signed on to *Young Intrepid* because Hollow was supposed to be the next up and coming dreamscaper, as they called all of the directors who took cinema to new heights with the innovation of brain trajectory recall technology. To utilize a person's ability to lucid dream for entertainment—this is what the craft of acting had become.

"Ms. Wallace?" a voice squeaked behind me.

I turned away from the poster of *Under a Tourmaline Sky* and saw her, standing with a clipboard and headset perched on her blonde locks, much shorter than I'd pictured.

"Daisy," she said, extending her hand. "Associate producer on *Wildfire*. Pleasure to have you on board."

She didn't need to mention that she was Hollow's wife. Her cold gaze spoke its own language. I cracked a smile, mimicking her contorted, high-cheeked grin. She squeezed my fingers together as if trying to grind the bones.

"The pleasure is mine. When Hollow told me about the project I was instantly interested."

"Yes. He's certainly glad that you could be a part of it. He's quite partial to you." She released my hand and wrote something down in her clipboard.

"I've heard a lot of wonderful things about you." I tried to glance over to see what she was writing.

"Forgive me, Virginia, but I have to admit there is something on my mind. The tabloids. From last year. I'd be lying if I said that the media didn't get to me. That I'd practically lost my mind with jealousy. Hollow told me that nothing happened between you two, but I just had to bring it up. I do hope you can forgive me."

"The paparazzi are out for blood," I said. "Hollow and I became close friends on *Young Intrepid*, but that photograph was truly blown out of proportion, Daisy. I'm sorry if something so trivial got in the way of your marriage. I assure you that nothing happened between us." I wished lying hadn't become so easy for me.

"I'm probably being too sensitive about the whole thing. Thank you, Virginia. It means a lot for you to be so empathetic."

"Anyone would have a right to be suspicious in your situation." I didn't know how much longer I could keep my cool.

She turned toward the corridor leading away from the lobby and deeper into the facility. "We have your dressing quarters ready, and your own sleep chamber to assure that you have all the privacy you need while in the lucid performance. Nothing but the best for our star."

I didn't want to be her star. She wasn't supposed to be there at all. *We split*, he'd told me over the phone. Two days of travel and nothing but reciting his lines, becoming Amber Hardley. I followed Daisy down the corridor, passing more posters lined along the walls, and imagined the next addition to the gallery. A ferocious snake outlining the close-up of my ghastly, horrified face.

∽∾∽

I should have turned around, forgotten about *Wildfire* and Hollow, and moved on to the next project. The next lover. Did Daisy know what he'd said to me over the phone? She was the last person I'd expected to see on set. I couldn't help but wonder if she'd become producer before or after Hollow called me the morning I woke up to the blaze in the Valley.

While waiting for the table read, I kept my distance from Daisy, gravitating toward the craft services table, mingling with oneirologists, lab assistants, and technicians. Not only did I want to build a rapport with the people who would be tinkering around with my mind, but I'd learned early on that people from the crew were humbled when the talent acted like regular people. One of them.

"I might be able to help you," said a man next to me, his paper plate full of fruit.

"I'm sorry?"

"With your disorder. The nightmares. Hollow told me all about your condition."

I could have shoved my plate in his face—if only for temporary retribution of Hollow's lie.

"I don't really like to talk about that," I said.

He put his hand on the small of my back, sending me reeling away. That's when I caught his magnificent blue eyes, chiseled jawline, pearly teeth. I remembered his face beaming front and center in several of the posters from the lobby.

"You're Lash Melbourne," I said. My mouth hinged, his name lingering on my tongue.

"We'll be performing in this picture together," he said. "I look forward to sharing a dream with you. Maybe later we can share a drink."

He walked away before I could respond. Before I could soak in the thought of co-starring in a film with Lash Melbourne, I saw Hollow for the first time since *Young Intrepid*. He was across the room, talking to Daisy. She caught me staring at them, carried on talking to Hollow, and batted one set of her pretty eyelashes at me.

∞

Water up to my waist. An island. The sand of an oceanic kiss sifts through my perforated mouth. I am anchored like dead weight to the shores of his skin.

I erode under his salty tidal hand. He smoothens my body until I am reborn. Glass. I cannot see his reflection in me. His hazel eyes are tourmaline stones—bound to shatter my fragile surface.

I have waited to be loved and finally with the hour upon us I allow the endless sand to spill through this wound. His serrated lips teach me the language of tenderness.

"Follow the trail of smoke," he says. "The embers will lead you to harbor."

∞

It took a few minutes for the real world to come back into focus. Before I was fully out of the dream, I heard Hollow's muffled voice outside the chamber, upset about something from the dream. I wanted to rip the electrodes from my head but my muscles were still numb.

The chamber door unlatched and Hollow stormed in, still smoking a cigarette.

"What's the big idea, Virginia?" he said, tapping his ashes on the concrete floor beside my bed.

"Don't know," I muttered, "what you mean." My tongue clung to my teeth as if I'd been anesthetized.

"I just thought we were all professionals here."

"Didn't I get all the dialogue right? 'Follow the trail of smoke, the embers will lead you to harbor.'"

"Oh, the dialogue was spot on. I don't even have a problem with the perforated lips. Nice improvisation. But how do you explain the fact that it was *me* kissing you, Virginia?"

I closed my eyes, clasped the last thread of the dream. The island. The kiss.

I have waited to be loved by you, *Hollow,* I longed to say.

"I'm sorry. It won't happen again."

"I have a lot invested in this production, Virginia."

"I know."

He leaned down to me, so close I could smell the tobacco on his breath.

"Maybe you could just pretend to be interested in Lash. Try a little method acting. If not, we could always increase the gamma—"

"I don't need an increase in frequency," I said, turning my face. "I just need to relax. Plus, it didn't help seeing you know who first thing this morning." I knew Daisy was in video village, notating the script with the other producers. Still, Hollow's eyes widened as if she could hear us talking under our breaths.

"I'm glad we had this talk," he said.

◑◍◍◍◍◍◍◑

The day they brought in the anaconda from the San Francisco Zoo, it took a team of thirty specialists to transport it. Talent and crew gathered in the basement of the facility where a tank was installed to secure it for viewing.

I had started to gravitate toward Lash. It was hard not to with his devastating good looks. Plus, I loved the way Hollow scowled any time he caught us together.

"What the hell is going on?" Lash asked, standing behind me while the team carried the snake to its temporary home.

Hollow entered the basement, clapping his hands.

"You all may be wondering why this enchanting creature needs to be here at this facility."

"Can snakes dream?" Lash asked.

"That is a great question, Mr. Melbourne," Hollow said. "I don't know whether or not snakes can dream, but I'm damn sure that you talented people can. Allow me to introduce your resident ophiologist and snake research specialist, Doctor Charlie."

The crew and team from the zoo clapped as a lanky man raised his hand to clarify that he was the specialist. It was hard to stay focused on him as he entered the tank with the anaconda by himself.

"Hello, I'm quite happy to meet you all," he said. "Your dreamscaper has asked me to educate you with some first-hand experience with the *Eunectes murinus*. That's just fancy Latin for big-ass snake." That got a laugh from members of the crew. As I looked around the room, I noticed that Daisy was nowhere to be found. Was she afraid of snakes?

"Roxie here is a thirty-nine-footer from Venezuela," Doctor Charlie said, stroking the green-gray coils of its tail. "She doesn't look it, but she weighs in at five hundred and fifty pounds. That's two hundred and fifty kilograms."

I wanted to get out of there, as far away from the beast as possible.

"I was wondering if your offer was still on the table," I said to Lash. "To help with the nightmares."

His teeth shone as he grabbed my hand and led me out of the basement.

∽༚∾

Lash took me to his room, decorated with statuettes of Buddha and bonsais lining his bathtub. He sat down on the floor, cross-legged, and looked up at me, signaling for me to follow with a tilt of his head.

I sat across from him, our knees centimeters from touching.

"I'm glad you came to me," he said. "I wanted to help you. First, put out your hand for me." I put out my hand. He took it in his, put my palm face up and drew a large half-circle with a black permanent marker.

"It's the letter C," he said. "For 'consciousness.'" He put out his own hand, as if waving, to show me the same marking on his palm.

"I don't understand. How is this supposed to induce lucid dreaming without gamma?"

"It's to help you test your reality. Start concentrating on the letter, on consciousness, and ask yourself, 'What is real?' By practicing this, making a habit of it, you'll be able to start testing reality while you're asleep. Always ask yourself whether you're dreaming or not. This reflexive attitude can be carried over to the dream state."

My hand lay cradled in Lash's, the *C* facing up. *Is this a dream?* I wondered. His grip tightened around my knuckles.

"Is it that easy?" I asked.

"I'm also a very spiritual person." My fingers parted, allowing his to interlace like a set of spiders' legs knitting a web. "I could show you that side of me. I would love to *truly* connect with you, Virginia."

꩜

In the desert, the nova's ghost refuses to gaze into me unless I'm naked. Consumed by soundless fire.

I resurrect him because I burn like the sun, rotating around his velvet plateau—a galaxy unlike any graffiti on Venus. I orbit him, an explorer, searching for meaning. The last green planet explodes with gunpowder—the kind with which his eyes set ablaze soulless worlds.

He may see the infinite symmetry in my scars, but the fragile constellations promise only a fraction of the hopeful distance between our feet and the stars.

I weep. It is Sunday and I count cicadas' cries in Rancho Mirage. The Milky Way effortlessly births the moonless summer night. The desert consumes me and his heat is paradise.

As the sand scorches the thin flesh of my back, I learn why men ignite for goddesses and dance blindly like sacrificial smoke toward the hungry sky, leaving the earth behind.

Shipwrecked.

꩜

I woke up quicker than normal, as if the gamma stopped suddenly rather than easing down slowly.

"She's in love with you, Hollow," I heard a voice say from outside my chamber. A crash of metal, a door slamming. "Aren't you? Aren't you in love with him?" A ring or warmth wrapped around my neck. Her hands. Daisy's hands. I was numb from the gamma. Her face came into focus and then rapidly pulled from my periphery.

"Don't touch me, you bastard. I'll put her to sleep. I swear it. I'll put her to sleep for good!"

"Don't talk like that, Daisy." I leaned up from the bed and saw Hollow and the oneirologist restraining her as she lunged toward me. "Get her out of here. Get her away from Virginia."

⁂

A draft blew in from Hollow's window. We sat side by side on his bed. After Daisy tried to attack me, I demanded an explanation.

"It was still me in your dream. There was no mistaking it. It was me you resurrected. It was me that floated up to the sky in that cloud of smoke."

"I don't understand," I said, looking down at the C Lash had drawn on my palm. "I could feel it. I could really feel myself inducing the lucid dream."

"She turned your gamma frequency up to one hundred and thirty hertz," he said. "I should have stopped her. It was too much for you. I understand if you want to leave the film."

"I don't want to leave the film. I want you to leave Daisy."

A shiver ran through my bare shoulders. Hollow stood up and covered me with a scratchy polyester blanket provided by the facility.

"It's not that easy, Virginia."

"I thought that's what *Wildfire* was about," I said. "That you'd left Daisy and wrote this movie for me. As a symbol of our love."

"I tried to leave her. I told her it was over, that we weren't going anywhere. Just spinning our wheels. I even packed a bag, Virginia. I walked out the door."

"Did you tell her about me?"

"I wanted to," he said.

"You told me that you and her were through."

"I knew there was no other way to get you here, to do the film."

"You lied to me."

"You slept with Lash."

I noticed the downward-pointing enclave of his eyebrows, the same expression he wore in my dream on the train.

"Are you a painter?" I asked. "I mean, do you paint? Or have you ever painted? Or have we had a conversation about painting?"

His eyebrows fell flat.

"I do paint. At least I used to. But not anymore, not in years. I haven't really told anyone about that. Not even Daisy. Certainly not you. Why do you ask?"

I closed my eyes and thought, *Is this a dream?*

"I want you to paint me," I said. "And then I want to destroy it before poisoning myself with varnish."

⌒⫸⫷⌒

The island again, only the water up to my waist is unnaturally calm. Gray skies swirl to black as an ominous crack of thunder promises deluge. We're both equidistant from the shore, and when he sees me, he starts toward me, moving at an unreal speed. Instead of swimming he glides, his torso never sinking below the water. There is no stopping him as he swirls around me in circles, a cyclone. Above us birds rise toward the sky—gulls, ravens, hawks. They cry by the thousands, their caws piercing in the enveloping darkness.

⚬⚬⚬

When I came out of the dream, I focused all my energy to my muscles, fighting the numbness from the gamma frequency. I reached for the wires protruding from me and pulled until all the electrodes were no longer suctioned to my head. The screaming still echoed in my mind. Once I realized that the cawing wasn't real, that the noise came from outside my chamber, I leapt from the bed. Sirens beamed, wailed within the facility. Technicians and assistants darted past me without a glance. I followed them, my legs still rubbery, and halted at the wall of people barricading the basement entrance.

I stopped at the sight of Hollow writhing on the floor, the serpent's jaw unhinged, its jowls around Hollow's waist. Suddenly, all the screaming and panic deafened. Absolute and total silence. As the anaconda contracted its thousands of muscles, Hollow flailed his limbs, smacking at the concrete, trying to claw his way out of the mouth. We all stood around and watched the attack from a distance, too afraid of the giant's power. Hollow's own jaw gaped, screaming, mouthing words. Finally, crew and specialists ran to him, four people taking his hands, eight more wrapping their arms around Roxie. I froze when I realized that the serpent was staring at me with one eye. Doctor Charlie said that there was no point, that there was no way to stop it. When I turned away from the unblinking eye, I collided with Daisy who stood transfixed at the sight.

"Let's get out of here," I said. "You shouldn't see this."

Her mouth hung agape, her limbs frozen in the contorted positions they took when she first saw Hollow in the snake's maw. I tried to pull her away but her body remained statue stiff. I couldn't just leave her there. I wrapped my arms around her and watched. As Hollow's legs disappeared down Roxie's throat, a sound like a canary's chirrup escaped from Daisy's curled lips. With the specialists fighting to separate Hollow from the beast, Hollow writhed with the vigor of a deity. A mythical creature. Half man, half serpent.

Separation Anxiety

*T*he day after I cheated on Andie, I woke up numb again from the medication. With the edge of a hunting knife I poked my finger until it bled, but still felt nothing. The scent of Anissa's sweat lingered in my sheets, mine and Andie's sheets. I covered my face in the linen and hoped to suffocate. After ten gasping breaths I knew it was a futile attempt. I got out of bed, chased my Prozac down with bourbon, and put on a pair of jeans.

Before I could get fully dressed the apartment door slammed ajar, blocked by the door chain.

"What's going on, Neal?" It was Andie, weeping on the other side. I couldn't just stand there half-naked; I had to let her in.

I undid the chain and stepped away from the door. I wanted to be as far from Andie as possible. Who knew what she was capable of?

"Are you okay?" she asked. "You have red marks all over your body." I gazed down at my bare chest. Andie was right. I must have looked like a cat attacked me. The marks were from Anissa's fingernails from the night before.

"Just an allergic reaction," I said.

"You don't have any allergies, other than dairy."

There was no arguing her. I escaped into the bedroom to cover my torso.

The sound of airplanes flying overhead came through the balcony window. I noticed sweat gluing my clothes to my skin, though I did not feel hot.

"I can't feel my skin, Andie."

She entered the bedroom and saw the blood on my hand from pricking my finger. Although mascara ran down her eyes and her blond hair was in total disarray, she had never looked more beautiful to me. She inched toward me, hand extended, Anissa's paintbrush dangling from it. "Did you stop taking the pills?"

"No," I said. "That's the problem. I'm still on the pills and I'm completely numb from any sensation."

"Let me take you to urgent care," she said. "And I know it was Anissa."

I pinched my hand to see if I could feel yet—still nothing. "It was Anissa," I said.

"I knew it." Andie dropped to the ground and sobbed into the carpet.

I don't know why I told her so bluntly. As she fell apart on the bedroom floor, I fought the urge to kneel to her and cry along. No matter how hard I tried I couldn't force the tears. With my lover of six years in a sobbing heap on the ground caused by my infidelity, I wanted to jump off our second-story balcony. It wouldn't have been enough to kill me—maybe just a few broken bones. But then at least Andie would see how sorry I felt.

"You had another woman in our home."

"I didn't think we'd come back here."

"You told me to go to a hotel and give you a night to think."

I pulled the shirt over my head, went to the kitchen, and sheared its polyester with a pair of scissors. Standing shirtless again, I opened the freezer, cracked the ice tray, and rubbed a handful of cubes against my flesh.

Nothing. I felt nothing.

I should let her take me to urgent care, I thought. The ice cubes melted in my hands. *They're like portable tears.* I went for my bottle of bourbon and found that I left the cap off when taking my pills. A couple of dead gnats floated around the syrupy, golden liquid. It didn't stop me from putting the bottle to my lips and gulping a mouthful.

"I think you should go back to Toledo," I said. "Your family needs you. Your sisters need you. You'll be happier there, Andie. We both know that."

"I need *you*." She crawled from the bedroom to the living room, unable to lift herself up. She was so helpless—so elegant in her defeat.

"You don't need me. You never needed me." I dropped down to her level, allowing the tears and drool to spill from my face. "Look at me. I'm a wreck, Andie. I don't know what to say."

Her eyes met mine, and her own tears ceased.

"I'll never forget this," she said.

I sprawled out across the living room floor while Andie stood up. She didn't speak another word. The door slammed shut behind her. In the rays of Los Angeles light, I splayed myself across the carpet and wept, clutching Anissa's paintbrush to my chest.

⌇⌇⌇

I waited in the bathtub for Anissa to arrive. By the time she got to my apartment my clothes were soaked and the suds had nearly spilled over the sides.

"Neal," Anissa cooed from the doorframe. Although she shook her head with her brows narrowed, I couldn't take my eyes off of her silky hair, sharp face, curvaceous body. Here she was, a woman I'd loved from afar, standing in my bathroom. I was a mess. I wanted to marry Anissa.

"This water is scalding hot." She pulled her fingers from the tub and stuck them in her mouth. "You have to get out right now."

I stood up. My clothes were stuck to my skin.

I had loved many women but never like Anissa. She guided me out of the hot water and into the bedroom where she stripped me. I wanted to feel my own naked body. I wanted Anissa to feel it, too.

"I might need urgent care, but I wholeheartedly believe that your love is medicine enough to heal me. I can't feel my skin."

Her hazel eyes weighed me down. I couldn't move under that goddess-like stare. "I'm worried about you."

"Anissa, I've known you for three years and although we've only been hanging out for a couple of weeks, I know that I want to marry you. I want to marry you as soon as humanly possible."

"You know what? You're right. You need to go to urgent care."

"I'm not joking. I love you. I need you. So, will you do it? Will you marry me?"

She contorted her jaw, sizing me up.

"I'm already in love with you," she said, shaking her head as if I'd just pissed the rug. "Give me a night to think it through."

⁂

The next morning, we chain-smoked outside the chapel until the priest was finished with the first Sunday morning ceremony. The owner had no problem taking walk-ins. I paid for the whole service on the spot.

"This really means a lot to me," Anissa said. She wore a jeweled headband over that dark, smooth hair. I envied the cigarette between her lips.

"I'm never going to regret this," I said. I had been more sure of that statement than I was of my own mortality. I had regained feeling in my skin later that night. Anissa had lain next to me in the dark, tickling my arm where the tattoos blended with the scars.

I felt her fingernails against me.

"Scratch hard," I demanded.

The sensation had been so overwhelming that I decided to skip my morning dose of Prozac. No depression, I had decided, was worth missing Anissa's indelible touch.

When the owner waved us inside, I took my bride by the hand and led her to the kitchenette-sized chapel room. There were no guests to witness us faithfully united. We tried to include our loved ones via Skype but my father and her mother both thought we were joking.

Standing across from me, the priest at our sides, I'd never seen Anissa so nervous. Her hands shook between my fingertips. Afterward, we made love all day, and when we woke the next morning, the window in Anissa's car was shattered.

"Why would someone do this?" Anissa cried.

"Is there anyone who would want to do this to you? Any enemies?" My first thought was that Andie had gone off the deep end. I could see her with a mallet and a ski mask, taking her rage out on the unwelcomed vehicle in *her* parking spot.

"Neal? Are you okay?"

Broken glass crunched beneath my feet. I looked into the car through the gaping hole to find Anissa's purse wide open, its contents splayed across the seat.

"I think she took your credit cards," I said.

"Who?"

"Andie."

"You think she could have done this?"

Back in the apartment, I called the Los Angeles Police Department to file a report. While waiting to speak with the detective, Anissa sat at my feet as if praying at an altar.

"She still loves you," she said, plucking a shard of glass from my jeans. "I need to know we didn't make a mistake." My hands shook while trying to hold the cell phone to my ear. Before I could answer her, the detective asked me what I needed to report.

Halcyon

We all have to do our share if Juno's Great Work is to be successful—this much I've learned. I'm not the only one breaking her back for the cause. I start each day cleaning the bunker where we all sleep, our cots in rows and separated only by hanging sheets. In the morning, after everyone has gotten dressed and left for their daily duties, I make the beds and pull down the sheets to open up the stuffy room. Once our bunker is perfectly tidy and sanitized, I head to the other side of the Sanctuary where people tend to the livestock, which, of course, are not for eating but for nurturing, breeding, and sustaining life. I cross a gated area where the shepherd watches over the goats, cows, horses, and sheep. He's a gangly man with a bushy beard and droopy eyes. We're in the same uniform—khaki pants and a green polo shirt. Beyond him stands the lighthouse, where Juno keeps the animals once they're ready to be tested for the Life Stasis Project.

This morning, the air is crisp. I breathe it deep into my lungs and feel a pep in my step. The memory of The Last Discotheque courses through me. We can't actually listen to music here—Juno says it is a passion we can only indulge in small doses. It's the one thing I miss most about my old life. Before going to sleep, I think about all of the auditions I've been on, the few gigs I was able to land. If there were Internet here, I'd pull up YouTube and look for the two music videos I was featured in, the ones my father hated because I looked "promiscuous." Sometimes I dream about my limbs being controlled by music. If I'm cleaning and nobody is around, I try to throw in a few moves, just to get it out of my system.

As I'm on my way to the lighthouse, I snap my fingers and attempt to moonwalk. I'm mid-shuffle when the shepherd catches me and smiles.

"Can't you just taste the clean mountain air?" he asks, his gnarled white beard twitching in the breeze. "And the ocean seems to be whispering, doesn't it?" I turn my head with him, pointing my ear toward the sea.

"It does," I confirm, wondering if he'll tell anyone about my secret dance moves. I lean over to pet the head of a lamb at the shepherd's side. I wish I had a job like his, protecting the animals instead of cleaning up after them.

"Duty is our bond," the shepherd says as I walk away.

"Duty is our bond," I echo, striding toward the lighthouse.

When Juno gave me the grand tour of the Sanctuary, he boasted that at 380 feet tall, the lighthouse is enormous compared to others along the coast. "It has four levels," he proudly exclaimed, "each recently renovated into top-notch research facilities designated for the Life Stasis Project." I have only seen the aviary and the laboratory, which are located on the ground level in an old fog-signaling building attached at the base. At first, the red and white brick stripes made me think of a candy cane, which made me think of Christmas, which made me think of home.

"This is your home now," Juno had said, as if reading my mind. "And you can consider this a permanent holiday. My gift to you."

Cleaning up after the animals is the hardest and ugliest part of the duty I've been given. At first, I tried to enter their cages with grace and tenderness. I tried to take pride in cleaning up their droppings, scrubbing their feces off the walls. Maybe it is the putrid smell, like compost and mold, that keeps me from taking pride in my duty. I'd tried putting a jumpsuit over the uniform, but it didn't make me feel any less like throwing up. Juno promised that I would learn to appreciate the animals in all their majesty. "Surely you'll be able to find your purpose and realize your destiny is intertwined with the animals—even their excrement." After Juno told me that, he cradled my head in the nook of his shoulder and kissed my cheek. "You have a wild soul, Alice," Juno said. "I know. I've seen you dance. I've seen your body try to create fire. Now is the time to tame your soul and give in to the harmony of the Sanctuary. Let the energy of this haven guide you."

The lighthouse alone takes half of my day to clean. The aviary is the worst level. Sometimes when I go to clean, the entire floor is covered with droppings and feathers. There are hundreds of birds—pigeons, gulls, hawks, hummingbirds, sparrows, loons, plovers, and dozens of other types. I enter through a special, netted door designed to keep the birds from escaping. Once I'm securely inside, the stench of shit and rot hits me hard. I keep my head tucked down, afraid of making contact with one of the winged creatures. During my first cleaning, a gray hawk had hooked on my jacket with its talon and wouldn't let go. I shook and screamed, which only made it peck me, drawing spots of blood around my wrist. It was Juno who had come to my rescue, distracting my attacker with a handful of sardines; he has a way of showing up at the perfect time, right when I need him most.

"You've got to show some force and authority," Juno had said, helping me up from the ground. In his kimono, he'd looked out of place, as always. Somehow, he'd been sparkling clean, not a single mark of dirt or grime. I'd admired this as he applied sanitizer to my wrist and wrapped it in a bandage. "They're not used to people. I'm the only human with whom they have contact. Purity didn't mean any harm. She just wanted to play. They get crazy in here. Could you imagine having beautiful wings like hers with no access to the sky?"

I'd brushed off my clothes, held my sore wrist, and looked over to Purity, busy trying to get the sardines down her throat.

I'm more prepared when I clean the aviary, now. Most of the birds have learned to leave me alone. However, there are a few areas I've been asked not to clean, for my own safety. On the topmost level of the aviary are cages containing larger, more exotic birds. Last week, the Life Stasis Project was given a donation of two birds on the endangered species list. Today, I can't resist ascending the ladder to take a quick peek into their cages. Purity flies up next to me and perches on the railing. I take a few slow steps down the rickety catwalk and, before I even see inside the cage, I hear a deep rumbling sound coming from inside it. I can already sense the bird's enormous weight, the ruffle of its wings slamming against the sides of its confinement.

I inch toward the front of the cage, my heart racing, Purity behind me quietly screeching, as if telling me to turn back. Before I know it, the massive creature is in front of me. I only get a glimpse when the sound of ABBA's "Dancing Queen" blares from my pocket. It's my ringtone, on a short loop of "having the time of your life." The bird stammers back at hearing this, seemingly anguished by the loud noise. It rocks back and forth and opens its beak, the caw like a fire siren. I reach for my phone and struggle to retrieve it through my jumpsuit. Purity flies above in small circles, unable to maintain her composure as the great bird tries to break free from its cage. The ringtone finally ceases, but it's too late—hundreds of birds frantically flap around. Their feathers and tufts of plumage circulate through the aviary. I feel droppings smack my hair like rain. I stumble back to the ladder and climb down, making a dash through a gaggle of raging geese until I reach the exit.

Outside, I fall to the grass and try to catch my breath. I'm covered in shit and feathers, terrified of what Juno will say if he sees me or finds out that I went somewhere off-limits. That's when I notice the shepherd staring at me. He and the baby lamb both appear to be laughing. I stand up and head for the showers, where I strip down and scrub my body until the skin feels raw.

After sanitizing myself in the showers, I go back to the bunker and check my phone. It had been a call from my parents that set off the endangered bird in the aviary. I haven't heard from them since announcing that I'd be living at the Sanctuary permanently. Juno has forbidden us to keep contact with anyone from our old lives, and he checks our phones regularly. I wonder what he will say when he sees their call. Will he praise me for not answering, or will he scold me for disobeying a major rule: "All technological devices are to remain in the bunker"? I consider deleting the record, but I put the phone underneath my pillow where I intend to leave it for inspection.

I decide to let Juno see the call, hoping it will only prove to him my devotion.

⟨⟩

The first time I go back to the lighthouse after the incident, I spend as little time in the aviary as possible. I can barely tolerate the smell, and fear that the birds have grown to resent me. Even Purity keeps her distance, perched on the farthest railing from the entrance. When I finish, I head down to the laboratory. It is not as repugnant as the aviary, but all of the science stuff gives me the creeps. There are rows of tables and workbenches systematically covered with beakers, Bunsen burners, petri dishes, and microscopes. I'm emptying the biohazard waste receptacles when I notice one of the lab workers, Seth, staring at me. It isn't the first time I've caught him doing this. Seth's been here long before me, one of Juno's first followers. Seth introduced me to the other devotees when I arrived, and since then we've been on friendly terms. With his lab coat, safety goggles, and clipboard, he looks like he is analyzing me instead of his test subjects. Sometimes it feels good to have an audience. He strolls from table to table, verifying and crosschecking his research. Does he know about the ruckus I stirred in the aviary? He looks up from his clipboard, locks eyes with me, and smiles.

"Don't be embarrassed, Alice," he says. "Nobody said the work we do here is easy. Sometimes we sacrifice part of ourselves for the greater good. I'd argue that getting tarred and feathered is a major contribution to Juno."

"Word gets around fast," I say, trying to forget being covered in shit as I wipe a rust-colored goo from the biohazard receptacle.

"Just a little joke. I saw you running yesterday." He points to the window facing the courtyard. "You should see some of the messes I make."

"What do you do in here all day?" I can't stop myself asking.

"Every day we're getting closer to Juno's goal," he says, keeping his eyes on the clipboard. "I can assure you from the inside, Alice, that there is not a day wasted."

"So, what's up with all of Juno's animals?" I ask. "At first I thought this was a farm, but I actually have no clue what this place is for."

"Perhaps not a farm in the agricultural sense," he says. "But we are harvesting data pertaining to all different aspects of life."

"So, you're harvesting data about animals? Like zoology?"

"Not quite." He smiles, looking up with a glimmer of excitement in his eye. "It's quite fascinating, when you get down to it. Juno's vision is on another level. You hear about people who changed society, technology, civilization. Bill Gates. Einstein. Galileo. Steve Jobs. Copernicus. Juno is up there with them. From the data I've seen and helped organize, I can tell you that when Juno reveals this project to the public, the world will change."

"I've only heard about the Project's mission briefly," I say. "Juno tried to explain it to me once, but it was a bit over my head."

"He can be very cryptic whenever he speaks about the Project. And he has every right to be. His work is so innovative that, if it went public too early, people would label him as a fraud. Or they would recognize his genius, steal his ideas, and advance them before we could."

"If you were to impart a few of the secrets, maybe it would help me fulfill my duty," I say. "Sometimes I have no idea what's going on, or what I'm doing. I just feel so clueless."

"I've sworn not to share many of the things I know," he says. "Juno has put his trust in me."

"And you can trust me," I say, instantly regretting it. Maybe I've been more desperate for attention than I realized.

"Tonight, then. After the ceremony." He looks up from his clipboard, the fluorescent lights reflecting on his goggles. "While everyone is having dinner, we can step away for a moment. We'll meet in the aviary."

"Sounds good," I say, gathering my sponge and bucket of soapy water. "I have to be on to the next stop, though. The Sanctuary won't clean itself."

"Right," Seth says. "Duty is our bond."

I start to walk away, but I pause, trying to convince myself that we haven't just crossed a line. Alone time without Juno's consent is forbidden. We are restricted from socializing outside the jurisdiction of our appointed duties.

༄༅

We all crowd together in our seats after filing in through the mansion's arched Victorian entrance. The buzz of love and purpose permeates the air. In the dining hall we face the roaring fireplace, in front of which stands a tall podium, like an altar, overlooking the crowd. Juno enters from his study with his chimpanzee, Maurice, perched on his shoulder. When we all see Juno, the room fills with claps and whistles. In seconds we're all on our feet applauding until Juno quiets us and motions to take our seats. I scan the room and search for Seth, but I don't see him anywhere.

"My beautiful brothers and sisters," Juno begins. "It warms my heart to see all of you together, joined in harmony." Maurice, the chimp, crawls down from Juno's shoulders and tries to run back into the study. Juno grabs Maurice by the wrist and says, "No you don't, you mischievous little thing." Maurice goes limp and returns to Juno's side, tame and sedated. The primate is well-groomed and dressed in a bright green tank top with cargo shorts.

"We are gathered to celebrate life," Juno continues. For the purpose of the ceremony, he's chosen a crimson kimono lined with golden threads. "Unity. In each other we have found a new home, a new family outside of what was given to us at birth. We have come together for the same cause and to find peace in each moment of our lives. I have built this Sanctuary and invited you all to come here so that you may have plentiful opportunities. I want you to experience this peace. This is true oneness. Once the pieces of the world blend together in your mind's eye, search deep within your soul and realize that it is not separate from your body. And your body is not separate from the universe."

Juno's smooth hands and face rise toward the ceiling, the orange light casting a shadow down his cheeks and neck. He looks around at each of us, even Maurice, who is pacified by Juno's words. With the glow of the fireplace behind him, it's as if he's radiating the light himself. "What I offer you," he continues, Maurice stirring with impatience at his side, "is the opportunity to earn oneness with no other attachments. It has been my life's work to create a sustainable place where only a select few may practice with me. I see before me life forms eager to discover the secrets of this existence. My promise to you is that, if you stay true to your purpose, you are on the quick path to unlocking those deep, sacred secrets. Duty is our bond."

We all repeat in unison, "Duty is our bond," stand, and embrace the person next to us. I turn to hug the shepherd, scratched by his rough beard. Across the room, I see Seth hugging Belinda, one of the cooks. His eyes catch mine as we both part from the people we're embracing. While everyone migrates toward the dining tables, I search for him, hoping we can eat dinner and forget all about our conversation this morning.

After a few minutes, the shepherd waves me over to sit with him and Belinda. Where is Seth? Is he waiting for me in the laboratory? Juno's words echo in my head: *Dining hour is the only permissible time to socialize.*

The shepherd stuffs his face with steamed roots. "Juno saved me," he says. "No job. No family. If it weren't for him, I'd probably be face down in the dirt."

Belinda scoops a heaping pile of vegan pasta onto my plate, says, "I was trying to be a writer. More like a waiter. When Juno found me and told me about this place, I knew it was the life for me."

As pesto drips down my chin I take another mouthful of the earthy food and the commune's chatter is interrupted by a piercing scream.

I stand on my tiptoes to look over a group of heads and see Maurice hanging from a chandelier, a poker in his hand thrashing at anyone who comes near him.

"Don't touch him!" Juno cries, shoving down Roger, the gardener and Carmella, the seamstress, in order to get under Maurice. "Come down, my baby, you come down here right this instant." Tears and spit are smeared across Juno's flushed face, his arms flailing around him in a rhythm of rage and fear. We all circle around him and the chandelier, keeping enough distance as to not be struck by Juno or Maurice.

The chimp starts to swing back and forth on the chandelier. His face contorts, eyes wide with rage as he points the poker straight down at Juno, and releases another piercing scream.

"Stop it, Maurice," Juno cries, falling to his knees and lifting his arms to the primate as if it were a deity. "I'll do anything. I'll give you anything. Just please come down from there."

Maurice flings the poker to the ground where its sharp edge juts into the hardwood floor. He jumps down, his face now mournful, sullen, and slowly paces over to Juno. Juno cradles the primate in his arms and faces the crowd.

"My apologies," he says. "Maurice would like you all to forgive him. He's been having a tough time since the procedure." Maurice's face goes expressionless as Juno says this. I don't know what procedure he's talking about, but many of the heads in the group nod in understanding. I assume they're more familiar with Juno and Maurice's relationship than I am. Juno takes Maurice to his study and closes the door. We all wait in a moment of anticipation, hoping that Juno will reemerge, but when it's clear that he's too riled we return to dining hour.

"I've always known Maurice wasn't tame," the shepherd says, sitting down to his plate of steamed roots. "I wish Juno would be more careful." I nod and look around again for Seth, but I'm certain that if he didn't leave before the outburst, then he's gone by now.

"Excuse me," I say, pretending to head for the restroom. Once I'm clear of the dining hall, I head for the veranda and don't look back. I plan to make my way through the cold, quiet air of this California night until I get to the laboratory. However, as I reach for the veranda's screen door, I see a small body looking up at me. It's Maurice, on his haunches, chewing an apple. His eyes sparkle in the moonlight, staring at me, unflinching.

"Hi," I say, instinctively assuming that this mammal, like another human, will understand what I'm saying. He just continues chewing, not blinking, his head tilted as if expecting me to say more. He lifts his thin upper lip, exposing a sharp-toothed smile. I continue through the doorway, making sure not to make a sound when I close it.

༄༅༅

I never went to the lighthouse, and I'm not sure if Seth did, either. But the next morning, I'm on my way out of the bunker when I'm stopped by Juno. His crystalline eyes are on the brink of tears and his hair, usually tied back neatly, unfurls down to his shoulders in greasy clumps. "I'm so sorry to interrupt you during your duties," he says, "but I was hoping I could have a moment of your time, please." Does he know that I almost snuck out last night with Seth? Or is it about my incident with the endangered bird in the aviary? At first, I stutter, trying to find the words without sounding stupid. He just stares, looking more helpless than I feel.

"Of course, Juno," I say. "I'm always at your disposal. Everything I do is in service of you and the Sanctuary."

He cracks a smile. "And I thank you for that, my friend," he says. "Please follow me to my study. I think it would be best if we spoke there, in private." He starts off toward the mansion without another word, and I just shadow behind him, keeping a distance of at least a few feet until we're across the courtyard and inside; Juno hates when people get too close without warning. Once we reach the study, he sits me down across from his pine desk and closes the door. The walls of his study are lined with books and collaged with maps, schematic diagrams, and x-rays of different animals. He releases a drawn-out exhale and gazes into my eyes.

"Alice, you know that I have brought you to this place, my home, as a member of my family. I took you in as you were, unconditionally. All I asked was for your complete faith and devotion to me. You wouldn't betray me or the Sanctuary, would you, Alice?"

"I would be nothing without you, Juno," I answer. "Before you, I had no direction. You've given me a home, a family, a life. I wouldn't do anything to jeopardize that."

"Good. We both know many people would sacrifice a lot to be in your shoes. But I chose you." He reaches across his desk with palms open, gesturing for me to hold his hands. I lift my trembling, sweaty palms and place them upon his. "There are some people here who are beginning to lose their way. They are going against my teachings. They are spreading lies. So, I am taking it upon myself to speak to certain people privately. You would tell me if something was wrong, wouldn't you, Alice?"

I freeze up, trying to keep my composure. "I would," I answer. "If someone approaches me and tries to turn me against you, I will come right to you."

Juno rises from his desk, goes to the door, and opens it for me. I stand up and prepare to walk out when Maurice comes running through the sermon room and into the study. "There he is," Juno says, taking the primate up into his arms. As he closes the door behind me, I wonder if Maurice somehow told Juno about my leaving the mansion after the ceremony. I must be insane to think that a little monkey would have ratted me out to his master.

Outside the mansion, I'm paralyzed with the realization that I should have looked for Seth. Instead of returning to my cleaning duties, I walk to the courtyard. The lighthouse looms in the distance, a shadowed tower reaching for the setting sun. I cannot spend another moment in the Sanctuary without talking to Seth. Not even the promise of Juno's oneness with the universe or the home he's provided can stop me from lifting my feet and racing past the shepherd and his lambs.

ᏇᎳᎳᎠ

The darkness inside the lighthouse blots out the Sanctuary's light. I push forward with fervor, going feet, yards, waving my hands in front of me blindly. I can't see anything but black when suddenly a small beam of light emanates in the distance. My hands search around and discover a handle, which I pull, unleashing a chamber flooded with a blue glow emitting from rows of capsules. The glass and metal chambers look like giant test tubes, filled with a liquid surrounding the subjects inside. My body freezes up. I tell myself to turn around, run back, confess to Juno that I've betrayed him and beg his forgiveness. But something holds me back. I need to know what are in the test tubes. I must see what Juno's been doing with the Life Stasis Project.

The stone floor is cold, the basement air stale and musty. I tiptoe forward, double-checking to make sure there is nobody behind me, that I'm completely alone. What would Juno do if he saw me down here by myself, blatantly disobeying his orders?

In the tube nearest the door floats a man, his eyes closed and arms crossed. In the tube beside him is a chimpanzee in the same position. The chimp looks like it could be Maurice's twin. As I continue down the aisle, I see more people I don't recognize—men and women, as well as animals of various species.

I want to vomit. Halfway down the aisle I feel my trembling legs about to give way. I'm not sure if the people I'm seeing are alive or dead. How long have they been floating in these tanks? How many of them were members of the Sanctuary, ensnared by Juno's lies? I reach the last of the occupied tanks, and when I look inside, the blood drains from my face.

Seth. His naked body, hooked up to the apparatuses and regulators. His eyes are closed, his hair sprawled out in the liquid. He's still alive. I retch, turn away, drop to my knees. I need to get up, move my scrawny muscles. I want to weep. Although this dark chamber is quiet except for the humming of the machines, I hear music in the back of my mind. The beat moves through me so vividly, I'd swear it was coming out of a speaker somewhere. First, I tap my fingers to the beat on the cold stone ground, and then I feel my heart synchronize. I force my feet to hold my weight and bring myself up. I breathe deep, prepared to make a move, when I hear the sound of metal screeching outside the chamber.

My first instinct is to go to Seth's machine. I search for a way to open his capsule and free him before it's too late. I know that the screeching must be Juno entering the lighthouse, and I estimate only a few moments until he's discovered me. Seth's machine doesn't budge even when I attempt to pry the glass from the metal with my fingers. The music continues, a constant vibration, even as I am grabbed from behind. I gasp for air, my throat swelling, and the music stops.

෴

I open my eyes and light floods in, an immediate and searing splice that goes straight to my brain. I close them and find but a fraction of solace when I notice the thread of fiery pain in my back. My body is limp, but I couldn't move even if I had the strength.

"Finally, you are awake," a voice says. It belongs to Juno; I don't need to open my eyes to know that. His fingertips land on my jaw, and I jerk away. A quick, axe-splitting surge of pain engulfs my spine, my shoulders. I open my mouth to scream but my lips are stiff, as if sewn shut. "I wouldn't move too much," Juno continues, tracing his fingers across my face. "Your body needs to relax. Any stress or force will only hurt you more." Somewhere else in the room I hear a sound, hollow and sharp—*clack, clack.* I try to open my eyelids but only take in blurred shadows before I must shield my eyes again from the light. "You've undergone a procedure. Honestly, I wasn't sure if you could endure it." *Clack, clack.* The sound repeats like wood against stone between Juno's words. "You have done a service for the Life Stasis Project. When I met you, I knew you'd be special. You were once lost and hopeless, and now you are fulfilling your destiny."

Fighting is useless. My body can barely endure the pain as I slip briefly out of consciousness. Darkness encompasses me. When I come to, I let my body succumb to the swelling and all-consuming pain. Juno's words play back in my thoughts. I try to discern if Juno is still here; the thought of seeing him makes it harder for me to open my lids, but I can no longer resist. I pull my eyelids apart in increments, letting the light spill in fractions. Either there is less light, or my eyes have grown stronger since I blacked out. I am able to keep my eyes pried open for a few seconds, taking in a window to my left and a figure directly across from me. I want to call out to it, see if it can hear me, but my mouth feels like it has been ripped from my face every time I try to speak.

My eyes snap shut. Once I can open them again my sight is a little more focused, and I strain to realize that the figure is strapped to a table like me. It sees me looking and twitches its head. *Clack, clack.* Is it trying to communicate?

Everything in my line of sight has come into clear focus. The room with its decaying, curved walls. The skyline out the window with the ocean's waves crashing beneath it, fighting to claw the shore. The likeness of the figure across from me, too, becomes clear. As it sets in, that Seth and I are trapped in Juno's lighthouse, I see the surgical marks—fresh cuts sewn closed—and the monstrous alterations that have been made to Seth's body. His face, swollen around the new proboscis orifice, is barely recognizable except for the hair that hasn't been shaved from his head. At first, I can't make out what this new mouth is supposed to be, but then I look to the protruding masses stretched out on either side of him. They're his arms, bent and reformed into unnatural positions. But that's not all; beneath the folds of his arms, underneath the elbows, between his wrists and torso, are blankets of feathers quilted together. I study the shape of these reformed appendages, makeshift wings. The sharp pain from my back and shoulders course through me. Juno must have done the same thing to my body. I can't feel my arms and can't crane my neck enough to turn my head that far. All I can do is go limp and slip in and out of consciousness.

༄

The incisions and new appendages have healed and blended with our flesh. During the day we mill around the coop and learn to use our new wings with a physical therapy regimen Juno has designed for us. For two days, all we'd been permitted to do is walk around and slowly rotate our wrists and shoulders for no longer than an hour. A week later, we are given a small platform, off of which we can jump and feel how the air moves through our tertial feathers. I'm starting to feel comfortable in this new form. Juno brings us our meals, chews it for us and spits it back into our beaks. "Soon," he says, "your testing will be complete and you will be transferred to the aviary. Purity misses you, Alice."

Although Seth and I cannot speak, we are beginning to develop a new language, even beyond the *clack clacking* of our beaks. He nudges me with his head, the blue and saffron feathers of his crest brushing against my nape. This means he wants me to climb onto the platform and test my wings, push the levels of my endurance. But I can only do so much. I don't have as much energy as him, even though I spend our nights watching the sunset over the ocean before I fall asleep and dream about my parents, about dancing. I think back to when I was five, on stage in my first tutu, lost in the music—and to when I was ten, cast in *Cats: The Musical*. I dream of all the dance classes I'd taken in high school and college. In the dreams my bruises from countless hours of practice still hurt.

When I wake up, I catch Seth staring at me from the nest he's created in his corner, his head stuck between twitches. When he notices me looking back, he hides his beak in the scapular feathers along the ridge of his shoulder. After a moment he points his beak to the window. *Clack clack*.

He gets to his feet and tiptoes over to my nook, shuffles through the scraps of paper and blankets that I've made into a bed. Again, he pecks at my nape and cleans the mites from my feathers. With a nudge from his forehead into my back, I stumble from my relaxed position. I'm forced to get to my feet or I'll tip over. With the new wings and no arms, it is almost impossible to stand up after we've lost our balance. I can't help but inch toward the window; with each nudge, I grow terrified that he's trying to push me out. His beak opens and a sound escapes, deeper than a *squawk* but less comprehensible than a scream.

I can no longer remain trapped in the coop, in the light-house. There is no way to escape through the Sanctuary, and I don't even know how long we've been up here. Weeks? Months? There is no way to escape other than to fly. I nip at the freckled, piebald pattern of tan and sapphire feathers along his shoulder. In a moment, he's on his feet, pacing around the coop. Cool wind blows in and I feel its soft tickle between my feathers. I catch the scent of salt and fish in the air. The breeze circulates around us, momentarily confined in the coop until it dissipates to nothingness.

Seth and I take a seat by the window. Our feathers brush against each other. We listen to the calm song of the wind danc-ing atop the sea. With the help of the platform we are able to reach the sill, the frame of the window large enough for us to stand side by side. We turn, face to face, and wriggle our wings in preparation. Seth and I blink at each other in confirmation and sway our bodies toward the water. Soon, there is nothing beneath our feet. We rush toward the crashing waves, hoping that our wings will carry us.

Family Business

*B*efore leaving the house, Darryl told Zane to carry the cans of green and yellow paint. And if he ever wanted to grow up to be a man like their father, he wouldn't cry or fuss about it, either.

They lived out on a big stretch of Ohio country and the road leading from their house to Tannenbaum's Junkyard was a two-mile walk. It was a blistering day in July, a week after the works. Scraps of star-spangled papers and matchsticks littered the long, dusty road.

Every few feet, Darryl looked back to find her brother stopped, trying to collect the carcasses of firecrackers and bottle rockets from the ground. He shoved his pockets full of firework guts.

"Hurry up, you heathen!" she yelled. He picked up the paint cans, running to catch up.

"Why do I have to carry these all by myself?"

"Don't you want to grow up to be a man, like dad?"

"Dad's dead."

And it was the truth. Their father had been killed in a car accident on Christmas before Zane could remember, along with their elder brother, Bobby. Less than a year later their mother took up with another man, mister John Tannenbaum of the Pennsylvania Tannenbaums. He came along and adopted Darryl, Zane, and the first daughter, LaShae. They left Pennsylvania for Ohio where John could open his business, Tannenbaum's Junkyard, to support his new family.

"Give me that," Darryl said and took the green can from him. "And don't you pick up anymore trash off the ground. You were raised better than that."

He smiled and carried on down the road beside her.

⟡

"This is a family business," John had said to Darryl. "If the business is to thrive, it requires help from the whole family."

John's business was scrapping and trading. He bought old machines and vehicles, or fostered unwanted ones, reviving them in the junkyard to turn a profit. His latest project was a rundown school bus bought at the county auction. He rebuilt the engine and removed most of the seating to make renovations for a motor home, which he would sell for twice what he paid. The final touch was the custom paint job. Green with two yellow stripes on the other side: signature John Tannenbaum coloring.

Darryl had wanted to tell John to paint his own stinking bus, that their real daddy was waiting for them up in heaven. It was an inch from her lips, but she'd known why her mother had married the man. It wasn't because he was nice or handsome—God knew he wasn't. It was the money, and his want for a family to call his own. Their mother needed someone around to show her and LaShae the truth about men, and a father for young Zane.

For that, Darryl loved and honored her mother, and would keep her tongue held tight.

∽∞∾

They found the bus past rows of oily auto parts stacked high in mounds, a valley of shrapnel. The bus's insides were hollowed out, mostly empty, all the seats ripped away and scattered in the dirt with the rest of the junk. Darryl imagined the bus as a rotting skeleton of a giant, extinct beast out in some desert.

"First, we'll paint one side green," she said, "and while it dries, we'll paint the other side green. Once we're done with the second side, we'll paint one set of yellow stripes. Then we'll climb up on the roof and paint it. After the top, the second green side should be dry, and we'll paint the last set of yellow stripes. Then we get to go home."

Zane's face lit up at the thought.

The hot sun beat down on their necks and backs until finally their skin peeled into white flakes. After several hours the bus was covered in a dull green, yellow stripes on one side. Darryl and Zane were on top of the bus painting opposite corners when Darryl heard her brother scream. She looked around and couldn't see him, and when she looked down, he wasn't there, either. The sound of his cries emanated—he was down there somewhere, alive and possibly broken.

Darryl crawled down the bus and ran around it until she saw him there, face down in the dirt, his skin scraped red and ashy. The paint can had come down with him, his body covered in the dull green. Darryl checked him to make sure no bones were broken, and soon she knew it was just the shock of the fall that had him in tears. She helped him to his feet and before long his eyes dried and his breathing slowed, and she carried him on her back on the long road home.

⁂

Darryl prayed that nobody would be home so she could clean Zane up without them noticing. God must have been listening that day because the house was empty, no sister or parents.

In the kitchen Darryl wiped all the dried blood from Zane's knees and scrubbed the green paint from his skin. The paint, however, would not come out of her brother's hair, no matter how many times she washed it. She had been trying to soak the green out all night when she heard John's truck pulling up to the house.

Darryl knew that if her mother and John saw Zane's hair covered in paint, she would live with their punishment for the rest of the summer. She snuck him into the bathroom and told him to stay quiet, like a good brother. He kept his mouth shut as she took the scissors from the drawer and cut all the green out of his hair. By the time she was done, Zane's head looked like a lawnmower had been at it. But he didn't fuss about it, no—because she was his big sister, and she'd carried him all the way home on her back. He just smiled up at her, and she smiled back, and they swept all his hair off the floor.

Love Drugs

*G*ray would take the pill and stop loving his wife forever. Down the hatch, sleep it off, and wake up without the same fervent, relentless, crippling heartache. That was the brand promise. The legal formalities would follow—divorce, separating the belongings, moving out, moving on—which would feel effortless without the added pain of the affair. *I'm the one who cheated*, he thought. *I'm the one who should make this as easy as possible for her.* Any time they had discussed it, one way or another he found a way to talk Autumn out of leaving him. It wasn't because she didn't want to; she'd tried countless times to pack a bag, get in the car, and leave for good. They could never go more than an hour without him apologizing in circles, begging her to forgive him and come back. And she always did. He worried she would live with it like a wound for the rest of her life, unless he severed himself from her.

He took the pill out of the orange bottle and placed it on the coffee table. The little pink capsule sat there, the only item on the black surface, like a dead insect. Over the course of an hour and two beers, the sunlight crept in through the window, filling the dark room with a dim radiance. The pill's shadow grew and stretched into a shape much larger than the pill itself, rotating on the table's surface in sync with the sun. He put the beer bottle to his lips and sipped until there were just enough bubbles at the bottom to swallow the pill down with later.

When he'd seen the psychiatrist, she noted his weight loss— one fifty-five to one forty-three—in the span of a month since the visit to his primary physician. "You're a healthy man," she'd said, a woman with long silvery hair and puffy, sleep-deprived eyes. "What have you got to be depressed about?" He stepped down from the scale and turned to the mirror. The doctor was right, he looked good for almost thirty.

"I'm sure your wife is a very happy woman," the doctor went on, her tone matter-of-fact. "I'm willing to bet she loves you very much."

"But what will my life be like once I no longer love her?" he asked.

"It will be the same as before," she said, flipping through his paperwork. "Only, you'll be able to move on and think for yourself, without your emotions for her affecting your judg-ment. You could always try something less permanent, like a nasal oxytocin spray or patch. Something to help the truth come out won't hurt."

He had tried the spray before, but knew that this time he needed something stronger. The doctor wrapped a blood pres-sure gauge around his bicep and squeezed the rubber bulb, inflating the device until it was airtight against his flesh. "It all depends on the extent of your present attachment to her," she said. "Nobody can tell you what your life will be like. I'm a doctor, not a fortuneteller. I can tell you what the drug can and cannot do for you. I can see if your body can handle the drug.

But only you can decide if it's right for you. When you leave, I can give you a brochure of patient testimonials, if that'll make you feel better."

"I'll take one," he said. The doctor took his vitals and led him to the counter near the lobby door. She handed him a pamphlet and a list of marriage counselors.

"I wrote you a prescription for a single dose," the doctor said. "One pill. That's all you'll need. I say this to every patient who comes in here for this thing: Before you take it, make sure that it is absolutely, positively, no-other-way-about-it the only thing you can do. We aren't meant to have power over some things in life."

⌀﷽⌀

When he got home, he opened a beer and started reading the brochure. The testimonials were paired with photographs of people alone, or looking out bright windows, or sitting down with a cup of coffee and laughing with a group of friends. They all suggested a life made possible from letting go.

The testimonial next to a photograph of a happy couple holding hands read *This pill saved my marriage. After five years of pure matrimony, things got shaky between my husband and me. He started having to travel for work, and I developed a close relationship with a man from my job. I was so close to committing adultery with this man, and that's when I heard about the pill. After taking it, I never thought about that man in a physical or emotional way ever again. And it goes without saying that I stopped seeing him while my husband was away. The pill made me realize how much I actually love my husband. Instead of extramarital activities, I've taken to healthy hobbies while he's away that only benefit our life together.*

Another testimonial, a photograph of a man and his loyal golden Labrador, read *I wouldn't be here if it wasn't for this pill. I mean literally, I would have been dead. I was with a woman with a serious addiction problem; I got dragged right down with her. I knew if I didn't make a change, we would only hasten our inevitable deaths. She couldn't let go of me, no matter how many times I tried to end it. I'm not even sure if she loved me for me or because I enabled her to be so destructive. Now I'll never know. After I took the pill, I was able to say good-bye. I gave her a wad of money, let her keep our car and apartment, and went on with my life.*

Gray wondered what his own testimonial would say.

There would be a photograph of him standing still in a crowd of moving people, his upturned face painted with melancholy. *I cheated on my wife*, it would read. *I broke her heart. If I didn't take the pill, she would have gone on with the rest of her life in a numb depression because I couldn't let her go. This pill gave me the strength to finally set her free.*

On the back of the brochure, at the very bottom in micro-sized text was the disclaimer: *Warning—Effects cannot be reversed. Capsule is designed for individual patient needs (will not have same effect on different person). Proceed with caution.*

He wondered what the disclaimer meant about the pill being designed for individual patient needs. What would happen if someone else took his pill? Would this person stop loving Autumn? What if they didn't even know her? Would they stop loving someone in their life who filled a similar role as Autumn did in Gray's? What if some poor guy in a perfect relationship stopped loving his own wife? Gray imagined the innumerable situations that could arise from someone taking the wrong pill.

But it wasn't like he was going to *forget* about Autumn. She wouldn't disappear off the face of the earth. He just wouldn't love her anymore. He considered consulting the list of marriage counselors provided by the doctor. Maybe after he took the pill, he and Autumn could attempt to rekindle some kind of friendship. He felt so stupid. He'd cheated on her because he felt a little bored. Now he couldn't even bear the thought of being without her. What kind of monster was he, the kind who would keep changing his mind, pulling Autumn along until there was nothing left of her? He picked up the pill and held it in front of him, pinching the pink capsule between his index finger and thumb. She deserves a good life, he thought. There was still time to cut their losses; even if she couldn't accept it, he could sever this one tie for her. He opened his mouth and placed the capsule on his tongue.

∽∞∾

Autumn didn't want to go home these days. Instead, she tried to roam around Santa Monica Pier for as long as she could before returning to her husband. After leaving the restaurant, she'd changed out of her stained smock and uniform, and into a denim skirt and tank top. She had a two-hour window before Gray would call and wonder where she was. That was one perk of waiting tables; her shifts didn't have an exact out time, so her husband never knew when to expect her. Lately he hadn't left the house because he didn't want to give her any more reason to suspect him cheating. He'd be there, waiting with dinner and maybe flowers, hoping to make up for his fatal error and prove that he still loved her.

She couldn't forgive that easily. Every night she'd tried to forgive him, to accept his apologies and believe that she could trust him again. She had become good at hiding the ongoing pain with smiles and witty jokes. The hardest part of pretending she was fine was when Gray had tried to have sex. It had been the one thing she couldn't fake without bursting into tears. In the three months since she'd found out about his affair, he'd only tried once. "Not yet," she sobbed after pushing him away. He'd tried to apologize and save the moment, but before he could speak, she'd gotten out of the bed, pillow and blanket in tow, and went to sleep on the couch.

The crisp ocean air blew against Autumn's face, its effect cleansing as it coursed through her lungs. Life felt more tranquil with the endless sea in front of her and the maddening city behind her. It reminded her of home, how she used to stare out at the vast flatlands of Ohio and maroon herself on some unnamed country road. She'd have given anything to transport there in a blink of her eye, just in time to watch the cherry sun setting at the edge of the road's vantage point. But she couldn't go home, not even for a short visit. Her family wouldn't understand the unmoving depression that clouded her; she'd never told them about Gray's affair. How could she have? His actions weren't only an embarrassment to himself, but also to her and their relationship. If her family ever found out, they'd never look at him the same way again. They'd think her a fool for staying with him, say, "I told you so" and "That's the consequence of getting hitched to someone you barely know." Even if her depression eventually blew over (something she knew wasn't likely) and she, by some miracle, learned to forgive her husband, the public knowledge of their marital weakness would be too much to live down. She preferred to keep the affair between them and let the pain callus over until it consumed her entirely.

Like Los Angeles, the affair would be something she couldn't escape.

When the ocean's wind became too cold, she found it difficult to pull away from the vastness. Since she'd been gazing, the number of people on the pier had nearly doubled. She thought about taking out her phone and scrolling through the contact list of people with whom she'd long since fallen out of touch. Sometimes she preferred the fleeting company of hundreds of strangers to the brief, awkward meetings with old friends. The city had a way of changing people, herself included. Nobody stayed the same long enough for her to grow real attachments to them. Maybe that's why she'd said yes when Gray proposed after their first fight as a month-old couple. She'd thought marrying him would be a way to finally hold onto to something she loved forever, but he too had changed into someone unrecognizable.

As a crowd of fishermen and tourists gathered along the dock's edge, she unhooked her arms from the guardrail and merged into the clamoring sea of faces. Among them she could be someone other than Autumn, a sad girl from Ohio. She could forget she was recently married, and even more recently cheated on.

Along the pier, she walked by a mixed-bag arrangement of buskers—a singer-songwriter strumming his guitar and wailing into a microphone, a break dancer contorting and shuffling on a pallet of cardboard, a ventriloquist cat-calling her in a cartoonish voice—and tourists from all over the world, snippets of their conversations in Spanish, Mandarin, Russian, or a language she couldn't identify, making their way to her ears. The addicting anonymity of being lost in this bustling world made her pain and problems feel less significant. She continued farther down the pier, observing groups of families and friends seated for late lunch. The air smelled of salt, the stench of fresh fish, and grease from all the seafood frying in the surrounding restaurants. She caught herself smiling at the sound of one group's laughter, and instantly felt pathetic for feeling jealous of the joy of strangers. How long had she gone without feeling real joy? Before Gray, she remembered the same stretch of numbing depression, her dull life rambling on like a constant AM radio talk show. When Gray had entered the picture, all of that changed, at least until his fling. After that, it was back to relentless monotony, like a permanent anesthetic running through her veins.

She deserved to feel joy again, but these days if it didn't come from Gray, she no longer knew where to look. She had become so removed from her own life. Gray's presence, his love, and his energy—every part of him had intoxicated her beyond hope.

Toward the middle of the pier, she stopped in front of Playland, a glowing arcade that screamed a spectrum of sounds: whistles, clinks, beeps, high-pitched tunes. It drew her in, reminding her of the hours she'd spent in arcades as a child while her mother shopped and drank vodka from a Styrofoam cup. On the night she met Gray, she'd told him all about her alcoholic mother and the father she'd only met once. He'd told her about his sister's death.

Autumn walked inside the arcade, past a group of teenagers and a line of children running around the tall videogame machines. She put a five into the token dispenser. It shot out a mound of golden coins, each one clashing against the metal dish. She scooped them out, the weight in her palm bringing back a familiar feeling of temporary limitlessness. As she turned to scope out which of the hundreds of games she would play first, her phone buzzed in her pocket.

It was Gray. She purposefully clicked the ignore button instead of letting it go to voicemail. Keep him in suspense, she thought. It felt good to let him worry for once with no idea where she was or when she'd be back.

Within a minute the phone buzzed again, a text this time. *Hey, just wondering when you'll be done with work. I'll have dinner ready, your favorite [tomato emoji]. Love you [purple heart emoji].* She turned the screen black and went to the nearest video game, one with pixelated zombies and two mounted shotguns. She slipped two tokens into the slot, picked up the plastic gun, and cocked the fore-end. Just as the game was about to start, someone stood next to her and lifted the second gun from its mount.

"Mind if I help you kill the undead?" It was a guy, taller than her by a few inches, with auburn stubble on his jaw and a white, beaming smile. She felt her heart bump, blood rushing to her face.

"Not at all," she said, withdrawing two more tokens from her pocket and slipping them into the machine.

༄༅

Gray spat the pill onto the carpet. He ran to the bathroom sink to scrub out any of its chemical remains before even a microscopic amount could take effect. The pill had had a bitter cherry flavor, its taste evoking the guilt of cheating on Autumn all over again. How could he swallow it down and lose the most important part of his life forever? Yes, he had wronged her, but there was such a thing as redemption, right? Maybe Autumn would find a new strength and move on from the depression. He'd already broken her heart once, but wasn't it her decision to leave or stay? If she wasn't hopeful of their love reigniting, wouldn't she just leave?

Maybe he would talk to her when she got home from work, be straight with her. He'd tell her that he would rather her live happily without him instead of miserable with him. Maybe that would prove how much he actually cared.

He gargled five mouthfuls of mint rinsing solution, allowing it to burn his gums and tongue. Once he was certain there was no trace of pill residue, he opened another beer and took a long, fizzy gulp. He'd almost lost her again as a result of his inability to make logical adult decisions. On all fours, he crawled around the carpet until he found the pill under the armchair, corroded with dirt and hair. It amazed him that something so small was capable of making such a large change in his life. After dropping the pill back into the bottle and fastening the lid, he picked up his phone to check the time. Five-thirty, far past Autumn's usual out time. He tapped her name on his screen and put the phone to his ear—only two rings before going to voicemail. *Did she just ignore my call?* He took another swig of beer and reasoned that she was probably caught up at work. It was a mistake to call her anyway; the last thing he wanted was for her to think he was desperate or insecure. She needed to see him with a constant air of confidence, even if he did worry about her exacting revenge while he tried to prove his steadfastness. Sometimes the thought kept him awake, especially the nights she'd slept on the couch. He'd lie with his eyes pried open to the darkness, imagining her face illuminated by the dim glow of her phone as she texted every attractive male contact about her current state of loneliness and despair.

The thought of her with another man was enough to slowly kill him, even though she had never been the promiscuous type. Still, he'd rather seem too desperate than not desperate enough and lose her to someone else. He figured a text couldn't hurt, just a quick "love you" and, to bribe her, he offered to whip together shells and cheese with her grandmother's homemade sauce recipe.

While boiling water, Gray thought about their one year of reckless romance and passion, the kind that only comes around once. Staring into the little flame on the stove, he thought about Darla. He'd slept with her once, at a wrap party for his first feature film, and waited two weeks until confessing to Autumn. He'd purchased over-the-counter oxytocin spray to help him get the truth out, and almost wished that the anti-love biotechnologies had never become such common pharmaceuticals. First a truth serum you injected into your nasal passage, and then a pill that could make you stop loving someone forever. What would they think of next? Before people knew it, Gray thought, love would be a universally synthetic experience. Everyone would forget about passion or cosmic connections in favor of emotional convenience.

He couldn't help but wonder if this would be the last meal he'd prepare for Autumn. He carefully diced tomatoes and blended them into a sauce with garlic, onion, and mushroom—every ingredient measured exactly to her grandmother's handwritten recipe. He dipped his finger into the sauce and licked it clean, the fresh, herby taste reminding him of when he met Autumn's family in Ohio. With flavors of garlic and onion still on his tongue, he left the stove burning, walked to the pill bottle, opened it, and put the pink capsule into his mouth. He couldn't go through with it before because it felt too final. But now, thinking about how he let Autumn's family down, it was enough to make him finally swallow the pill. It was in his bloodstream by the time he returned to the stove. He plated their dinner and cleaned the dishes. He left the kitchen light on for Autumn and went into their bedroom where he fell asleep, praying he'd wake up without an ounce of love for her.

⟨∞∞⟩

When Autumn got home the apartment was dark, except for the kitchen. The smell of fresh garlic filled the air as she turned to find the table set for two, flies buzzing around the wine in the decanter and stale shells left on their plates. She waited a moment, watching a fly dive into a shell's opening, out of which spilled soft, white ricotta. Silence, except for the faint buzzing from the insect. Autumn kept still a moment to see if Gray would come greet her, or if he was already asleep in the bedroom. Surely, he wanted her to see the wasted meal he'd prepared for her—another small guilt trip to prove how hard he'd been trying to make things work.

She turned off the kitchen light and tiptoed into the bedroom where she saw Gray's body under their blankets. She was naturally inclined to move around noiselessly to prevent waking him. Instead of putting on her pajamas and slipping into bed with him, she went into the bathroom and sat down in the dark. Had she truly succumbed to such temptations of the flesh? Or was it a lust for revenge to which she could not yield? Never before had she made such a costly spur-of-the-moment decision; its gravity pressed her down into the cracks of grout on the floor. She wondered if Gray's decision to cheat had also been spontaneous—a flight of unwieldy passion—or if it was premeditated. What if the stranger had never entered the arcade? Would she have still found a way to sabotage what thin tendril of love remained between her and Gray?

When the thoughts of kissing the arcade stranger became too much to handle, she distracted herself by withdrawing her phone and pulling up Darla's social media profile—anything to take her mind off the guy's menthol breath and scratchy facial hair. Autumn liked to look at Darla's profile and scan through her pictures, seeing all the updates of her life. It was addicting, the envy that came with constantly comparing herself to the woman with whom her husband had slept. Before Autumn knew it, an hour had passed staring at Darla's photos—her amazing job and apartment, her perfect body—all the things that Autumn could never give Gray.

She'd thought that kissing the arcade stranger would have finally rid her of the jealousy she felt for Darla. However, sitting there in the bathroom, the tub's constant drip ticking like a clock, she realized that cheating on him didn't relieve her at all. What was she supposed to do with this revenge now that she cradled it like water in her hands? Would she drink it down and keep the truth buried forever?

She replayed the entire event over in her head—every improvised gesture and touch—and decided that she would tell Gray. But she couldn't go at it alone. Given her penchant for passivity, she'd most likely make something up at the last minute in order to avoid any conflict. To ensure that she would go through with it, she'd need some medicinal reinforcement to settle the matter for good.

She self-administered the synthetic oxytocin spray with every intention of saving her marriage. With Gray still asleep in bed, she snuck the prescription bottle from the back of the junk cabinet and squirted the chemical up her nostrils. The sun would soon hang over their beachside apartment. Gray would wake and the bond-enhancing substance would circulate in her brain. She told herself that she would be able to forgive him, that the oxytocin would help her move on. Mothers use it to get their children to bond with them, she reasoned. Why shouldn't it work for spouses just the same? She looked at her tired, droopy face in the toothpaste-splattered mirror and turned off the bathroom light.

The sun had just begun to shine through their crimson curtains. Gray lay facing the wall, still at peace in a deep slumber. Autumn sat down on the edge of the bed and rubbed her hand up his leg. She felt a sensation like water running through her head. It was the oxytocin taking effect. "Honey," she said, her fingers now patting his brown, matted hair. "My love. Good morning. You're my world. There is something I'd like to talk to you about."

Gray slowly turned from the wall and gleamed at Autumn through squinted eyes. "Tell me," he said. He remembered the pill, and that he once loved her. "Tell me everything, but it won't change a thing."

Taking Flight

Before I died, I was just trying to be a normal teenager. While a lot of the kids at Toledo Technology Academy went to the Robotics Team after school, my best friend Athen and I preferred to mingle at the Westfield Mall with girls from other schools. The only four girls in our grade at TTA dated upperclassmen. Desperate to find girlfriends, Athen and I perused the food court and hip stores to gain perspective on the regulars. They were mostly from public schools and they stuck together in their respective cliques—preppy, sporty, religious. But then, there were the outsiders. The nerds and the artists, vocational school girls on the fringes of normalcy. I was most drawn to the art school crowd, who dressed in all black and wore concealer with pearl powder. Athen and I were still in uniform, green polo and khakis. There was a part of me that knew I would fit in better with the art kids than I ever could at my own school. I had no place studying robots at the technology academy. Art was in my soul. I envied those other students who learned to create art, not machines. I wanted to infiltrate their space, become one of them.

Being dead is like binge-watching an adaptation of your life story. All you do is watch this other person say all of the stupid or meaningful things you said. My adaptation begins when I met the girl who changed my life. It was the third week of September, sophomore year.

"Three o'clock," Athen said. "Theatre kids. New girl. She's *definitely* a man-eater."

I snuck a three-quarter-turn look her way, making eye contact from across the packed dining area. She had fair skin, ash brown hair that met her shoulders, and green eyes like a forest at sunset.

"She's looking right over here," I said. "If I don't make this girl fall in love with me, I'm going to die." Isn't life ironic?

"You're the most dramatic person I've ever met," Athen said, shaking his head. "It's just like you to steal a girl right out from under me." As we walked toward the group, the girl looked up at me, and then looked away just as quickly. I could see her telling her friend that we were coming over.

"What's up, everybody?" I said, trying to be casual. "You go to the art school, right?"

"How'd you guess?" her friend asked, pointing down to her shirt that had *Toledo School for the Arts* printed above a graphic of a jagged hook and pirate ship. She was the taller one of the two, with jet-black hair and a nose ring.

"Cool," I said. "We go to TTA, but I was thinking about transferring to your school. I really want to be an actor, see." I glanced down right at that moment to take in a perfect, slightly crooked smile on the face of the girl with whom I had made eye contact. It wasn't just her natural beauty that drew me to her. I was equally entranced by the other things I had noticed about her, like her white Chucks, stained with sloppy handwriting in what looked like quotes and lyrics. I wanted to crawl down on the sticky mall floor and read every word on those shoes.

"Not just anyone can get in," Nose Ring said. She nudged my future lover with her elbow. "You actually need to have talent."

"How'd you get in?" I said to my new crush. "What's your talent?"

She looked up, shocked, not quite registering the fact that I, the really handsome guy with shaggy hair, a cool studded belt, and custom Vans, was standing in front of her and asking personal questions. Or at least, that's what I thought. I was so full of myself back then—when you're dead, you *really* see your old self through a new lens.

"Sylvia's got more talent in her pinky than you have in your whole body," Nose Ring said.

"Oh yeah, well my pinky knows *Romeo and Juliet* better than your entire theatre department," I said. "I'm a poet. Poetry is the art of moving language and it, like any other art, can be… performed!" I thrust my arms out in a grand gesture, mimicking so many actors I'd seen on the stage. Athen let out a sigh.

"There are puppets and there are actors," Sylvia said with her palm facing me, as if to reject my dramatics. "Puppets are controlled by the world. Actors have choice and free will. Right now, I'm thinking you're more like the former."

The girls and Athen all stared at me, waiting to see if I had a comeback. Not only was I absent of words, I'm also pretty sure I wasn't even breathing. I looked to Athen, who was too caught up smoldering at Nose Ring with his eyebrows arched. Sylvia's words burned through me. *Puppets are controlled by the world.* I'd found the perfect woman.

"I just met you, and I know we're both super young, but I would *totally* be down to marry you like right this second."

Sylvia stood up from her seat and looked me square in the eye. "I wouldn't lift a finger to save your life, let alone marry you. Let's go, Doris." Her stride parted a group of football players in line for pizza.

Nose Ring stood up to follow her, smirking at Athen and me. "Don't take it personally," she said. "Not every princess can envision themselves in your perfectly rehearsed high school fairy tale."

"You don't understand," I said. "I just met the girl to whom I will devote my poetry for the rest of my life. Like, you may very well be my muse, Sylvia!" I called after her. "No pressure, or anything. But, would you prefer a sonnet or a dramatic monologue?" My beckons rang unheard as she walked away. The girls faded into the swarming crowd.

"Look at this," Athen said. He picked up a handbill from the bench where Sylvia and Nose Ring had been sitting. I snatched it from his hands, reading the large decorative font.

PETER PAN

LIVE ON STAGE

PRESENTED BY

TOLEDO SCHOOL FOR THE ARTS

AUDITIONS HELD SATURDAY, OCTOBER 15

"That's it. I'm going to audition for Peter Pan and win her over," I said. I folded the flyer up and shoved it in my pocket.

"You probably can't audition," Athen said. "You don't even go to that school."

"I guess we're just going to have to crash the auditions."

Athen laughed and patted me on the back. "That is the worst idea you've ever had."

⟨⟩

After meeting Sylvia, I paid little to no attention in class. I read and reread the *Peter Pan* novelization and play. If the teachers caught on to my lack of attention and forced me to participate, I would find a way to dedicate my work to Sylvia: in Automation class, we were assigned to program traffic lights to turn from green, to yellow, to red. Instead I programmed them all to blink red in a heart shape. Inside the digital traffic light heart, I spelled S-Y-L-V-I-A with stop signs. In Materials Processing, we were supposed to build a mousetrap-powered car and I named my pink contraption *The Sylvia 7*. It won the class race. In typing class, while everyone else hammered away in unison the keystrokes *F D S A SPACE J K L SEMICOLON SPACE*, I utilized my time to compose a twenty-page doctrine of love for Sylvia. *To you who captivated me in the food court*, it began, *I promise my undying devotion and tenderness. You make my otherwise dull world glow with your radiance. You are the only burning star in my heart's vast sky.*

⟨⟩

The morning Athen ran lines with me before the audition was the first time I looked to the sky and considered the possibility of flight. Peter Pan could fly with the help of fairy dust from Tinkerbell. Whenever I thought of Sylvia, a buzz coursed through me and amplified every step I took, every breath I drew. If Peter Pan could fly, why couldn't I? Love would be my fairy dust.

Walking through littered downtown Toledo, the Maumee River beneath us, I believed that if I leapt off the Cherry Street Bridge something magical would prevent me from hitting the dark, dirty water. I took the cold steel rail in my hands and hoisted myself up. With the wind grazing my back and the sprawling river before me, I felt like if I took a single step, I'd be suspended above it all.

"Watch out for Tick-Tock the Crocodile," Athen said, deadpan. "But seriously, please don't fall. I don't have the energy to save you."

"You should audition," I said. I climbed down from the railing. "You practically have the part of Captain Hook memorized." I unsheathed my Styrofoam dagger from my backpack and went for his throat.

He evaded the lunge and disarmed me of my dagger like a true pirate. "I don't think acting is really my thing," he said.

"Come on, bro," I said. "It's something we could do together. I bet you'll meet all kinds of girls. Maybe you can hang out with Nose Ring."

"Nose Ring? Her name is Doris, which you might have overheard at the mall if you weren't so in your head all the time."

"I'm still not sure how I plan on asking Sylvia out," I said, reaching for the dagger and steering the topic back to my most pressing concern. "Our first encounter was pure—spur of the moment, completely spontaneous. This time, she'll see me at the audition, recognize me, and know that I'm there for her. To make her see me."

"She didn't seem to be that into you at the mall," Athen said, forfeiting the dagger. "What if she sees you and thinks you're desperate?" It struck me that Athen might have been jealous because

I went after Sylvia right away. But who was he to stand in the way of true love?

"I know you saw her first," I said, starting to cross the street. "But I don't want this to come between us."

"Despite what you may think, Sam—" he stopped in the middle of the intersection. Cars zipped around us. "—the world does not revolve around you."

When I was alive, I thought Athen envied my bravado and charisma. If envy were possible in death, I might wish I had had more of Athen's sensibilities: candor and realism. It wasn't until after the accident that I understood what he meant that day on the bridge.

The Toledo School for the Arts looked more like the sarcophagus of an industrial building in the heart of downtown Toledo than an educational institution. The closer we got to the school, the more I feared I'd throw up. Sure, I kept cool on the outside, but inside, I was a wreck. I kept imagining Sylvia and the rest of the art kids laughing at my pathetic attempt to audition. I told myself to pretend I was as cool as James Dean in *Rebel Without a Cause*. I adjusted my beanie, threw my hands in my pockets, and walked through the doors like I was a real Hollywood icon trying to be modest.

The inside of the school smelled like oil paint and sweat; it was alive with creativity. We meandered through hallways with walls covered with art for a good ten minutes before we found the right room. I wondered if any of the art was Sylvia's and tried to find a sketch of my face among the portraits. I could have wandered those dingy hallways forever, looking for my likeness on the wall. Finally, we saw the flyer with the pirate ship and jagged hook. I expected a desk where I'd fill out information, but it was one giant black theatre room with a bunch of kids sitting on metal chairs watching the one on stage who was delivering a monologue. The door slammed behind me and everyone shot around to look at us. That's when I saw Sylvia sitting there, in the same outfit from last week. I could barely keep myself from running over to her and reciting an excerpt from my love doctrine. When she registered who I was, she flipped her hood to cover her face and slunk down lower in her chair.

"To what do we owe this pleasure?" a gray-haired woman in a black dress called from the first row. I assumed she was the director of the play.

"I'm here to audition," I said. "Is there a signup sheet, or—"

"I have never seen your face before in my life, child," she said. "Do you attend the School for the Arts?"

"That's the thing," I said. "On the flyer for the audition, it didn't say anything about being a student here."

"Well, I'm afraid you must be registered at this institution in order to perform." She lowered her glasses back down onto her bony, forlorn face and turned to resume the audition. Before the actor on stage began again, I stepped forward.

"But this isn't a private school. Students from all over the city go here, right?"

"Correct," she said, turning back around. I could see Sylvia trying to become invisible. Why would she be embarrassed by me when, just the other day, I so valiantly confessed my admiration for her?

"Then, like sports programs, students from other schools should be able to try out, right?"

She flipped her hair, eyeing me up and down. "And what institution *do* you attend, child?"

"Toledo Technology Academy, ma'am," I said. The students chuckled, which only fueled my need to show them what I could do.

"Do you have any *experience* in the thee-ay-ter?" she asked.

"I acted when I was a kid, and I know this play front to back."

"Oh, so you were a child actor," she laughed at her own joke. "Then you must be eager to dazzle us." This made the students laugh harder. I noticed Doris sitting a row away from Sylvia, sniggering.

"You are *in* for it now, Romeo," Doris said.

"Well, child," the director proceeded. "If you are so *inclined* and *inspired* to interrupt my audition because you *lust* for thee-ay-ter—then by all means step forth and grace us with your magic. Light up this room with your symphony. Show us what you got."

"Right now?" I said. I looked up to the guy on stage whose audition I botched.

"Well, go on," the director said. "You've already altered the aura of the room with your paper-thin machismo."

"Seriously, Mrs. Chabbock?" Doris pleaded. "You're going to allow this pretentious faker to waste our time?"

"Even fools deserve a chance," Mrs. Chabbock said. I could see Sylvia tightening the cord of her hoodie until it scrunched around her face. I walked past the grid of metal chairs, jumped up onto the stage, and took the place of the guy before me. It felt as though my heart was hammering against my rib cage. With the stage lights beaming in my eyes, all I could see were the vague silhouettes of the kids in their chairs and Mrs. Chabbock across from me, her eyes wide and wicked as if she expected me to summon the devil.

I turned around to face the curtain. Even then, I knew how cliché I looked—a know-nothing actor. But I had once seen James Dean do it in a documentary. To get into character he would turn away from his audience, close his eyes, and return as someone new. When I pivoted back to face the audience, I felt my body detach from my soul.

"Yes, Wendy, I know fairies!" I cried. "But, they're nearly all dead now. You see, when the first baby laughed for the first time, the laugh broke into thousands of pieces and they all went skipping about, and that was the beginning of fairies." I looked across the audience, not breaking character, so that I could gauge their response. Just like I thought—cold silence. "So, there ought to be a fairy for every boy and girl. There isn't, of course. You see, children know such a lot now. Soon as they don't believe in fairies, there is a fairy somewhere that falls down dead." At this point, Peter Pan realizes he can't find Tinkerbell. But something came over me. I changed the line so that Sylvia would know once and for all what this was really about. "I can't think she is gone. Sylvia, Sylvia, where are you?"

Then, as if Peter Pan had taken complete control of my body, I leapt off the stage, flying toward Sylvia, and landed with a half-roll to my knees and into a bow. When I stood up and looked toward the crowd, I expected them to explode in applause, but all I heard was Doris saying, "Please, somebody spare me."

Sylvia bolted up and stormed out of the dark theatre, Doris chasing after her.

"Sylvia!" I cried. "Wait!" I ran across the auditorium and through the door.

"They can't be far," I said to myself. I started sprinting through the hallways, those makeshift galleries of student art, but didn't see Sylvia or Doris anywhere. I went outside and looked for them, but the streets were empty.

"She's gone," Athen said, coming up behind me and gasping for breath.

The decrepit downtown buildings surrounded us like the walls of a maze. I called out Sylvia's name as loud as I could. Nothing. Nothing but the sound of my own voice reverberating back.

⁂

I was feeling depressed until I got a call the next day from Mrs. Chabbock. "You, my child, *are* Peter Pan!" she wailed into the phone. "Of course, I had to bend some rules because you are not a part of this institution. No matter. You will lead this play with Sylvia Pryor as Wendy. You will not let me down. Rehearsals begin in a week." She hung up before I could respond. We both got the leads. Peter and Wendy, Sam and Sylvia.

I showed up to the first rehearsal in green tights and a tunic. "This isn't a dress rehearsal," Doris said from the stage. "You look like Mary Martin on the poster for the 1950s version of the Broadway production." The rest of the cast and crew laughed. Beside Doris, Sylvia looked like she was about to vomit. I felt embarrassed for her. Nobody else was in costume, just tee shirts and sweat pants.

"There he is. My Peter Pan." Mrs. Chabbock embraced me and eyed my clothes. "A little overprepared, but I wouldn't expect anything less from an actor with such intense emotions. Partner with Miss Pryor. Run act one, Peter's entrance." She nudged me toward the stage. It was the moment I had been waiting for—one-on-one time with Sylvia. When I walked onto the stage Doris yawned in my direction, staring at me while sanding the side of the pirate ship. I wasn't about to let her attitude ruin everything.

"How are you?" I asked Sylvia, ignoring Doris. "How is school going? Hey, do you have a boyfriend?"

"Is he serious right now?" Doris groaned.

"It's fine, Doris," Sylvia said. "Can we just get on with the lines?" She tied her hair back and avoided eye contact. It was my first time being so close to her, within arm's reach. Her scent, cigarettes and sugarplum, were enough to make me feel drunk. But I had to suppress my intoxication. This was my shot. I had my lines memorized, but Sylvia had imbued the entire script into her being. She finally gazed into my eyes as we circled the stage. The rest of the group gathered around us, unwilling to break our momentum. Once we got to the part when Peter teaches Wendy and her brothers to fly, everyone—even Doris and Mrs. Chabbock—was speechless.

Mrs. Chabbock stepped forward after an electric silence and faced everyone but Sylvia and me. "That is all for rehearsal today. We meet again next week." As everyone headed toward the exit, Mrs. Chabbock turned to us. "Your chemistry is undeniable. I know that I have cast the right performers. But do not let me catch one of you trying to upstage the other again." Her eyes jumped to Sylvia as she said this. "Theatre is a communal art. You will learn to view each other with respect." She stepped down from the stage and exited the room. Sylvia darted for the door. I tried to stay near her, like a shadow.

"Did you hear that? Our chemistry is undeniable." She kept walking with no response. "Sylvia—if you ever feel like rehearsing more, I wouldn't mind coming to your house."

She exhaled deeply. "School is just fine." I followed her down the hallways lined with portraits until we were both outside. She rushed to an old, rusted blue Buick idling across the street. The guy behind the wheel huffed on a cigar that looked too big for his rodent-like face. I wasn't sure if he was her father or what, because from a distance he looked maybe ten years older than us. I wanted to walk up to the car and introduce myself. I wanted to learn about her personal life. Once she was inside, she slammed the door and covered her face with her hood. It looked like the driver was yelling at her and laughing. I couldn't make out the words, but I started toward them ready to ask him what his problem was. When he saw me standing in the middle of the street staring at them, he hocked a giant spitball out the window and blasted his radio. The tires screeched as he pulled away.

Sometimes I pause the adaptation of my life's story here. I rewind and watch this guy spit at me again. In this instant replay, I notice a smirk on his face and a faded tattoo on his neck. I can't tell if it is the top of a question mark, or the pointed end of a hook. What would have happened if I had followed Sylvia that day? Maybe it all would have been different. Maybe I wouldn't have died. Either way, I had no way of knowing how important this moment would be. I felt that something wasn't right, but I didn't act on it. I was too busy in my own head, like Athen had said, too concerned with myself. I was still that puppet from the first day that Sylvia and I met. If I had made a choice to act, then maybe I could have saved myself. I wish I had a way of knowing if I saved her.

⟨⟨∞⟩⟩

Seeing Sylvia every week for rehearsal became the highlight of my existence. When we finally got to the scene where Peter Pan teaches Wendy to fly, Sylvia and I were both hoisted up by our harnesses. The equipment was heavy, clunky. While Sylvia retained perfect mid-air balance, I teetered from side to side, forward and back, in my struggle to glide over to her. When I finally reached her, I took her clammy hands in mine. As the stagehands tried to figure out the dolly, us suspended above everyone's heads, I kissed her fingers. She slapped me hard across the face.

After they pulled us down, the cast and crew chastised me for going off script. I stepped aside, trying to ignore their heckles while they reset for the scene I had ruined. That's when the pink pill bottle caught my eye. It was across the stage, in the darkness beyond the spotlight. When I was sure that no one could see me, I walked over to the shadows and put the bottle in my pocket. I couldn't really say why I did this. Curiosity, maybe? To whom did it belong? What kind of pills did it hold? I surveyed the theatre, but nobody, not even Doris, looked like they had just lost something important.

That night I had stayed late to rehearse my monologue when Sylvia wandered into the theatre.

"You look lost," I said from the stage. She jumped, releasing a sudden shriek.

"I could kill you," she said.

"I found something on the stage. It was right where we landed."

"What did you find?" The chasm between us amplified her voice, as if she knew how to manipulate the acoustics of the auditorium.

"Pills. A bottleful of different kinds."

"Did you take one?"

The bottle was still in my pocket.

"No," I said and held it out for her to see.

"Did you want to?" she asked, taking the pill bottle and twisting it open.

In the void of the auditorium, I couldn't resist her. I would have given anything to share a moment with Sylvia. She plucked a pill, half black and half purple, from the bottle, placed it on her tongue. She gave one to me. I wanted to ask what the drug was, but I didn't want to spoil the moment. For the first time outside of rehearsal, the eye contact she made with me felt inviting, as if I didn't need her permission to look back. When she swallowed the pill dry, no water, I mimed her.

"So, what's supposed to happen?" I asked. She took me by the hand and guided me up the steps of the giant, fake pirate ship. I looked around at the set—the clock tower, the hollowed-out trees of Neverland, the massive papier-mâché crocodile—and wished that all the make-believe could be our real life. Alone in the theatre with Sylvia, I felt as if we were trespassing and embarking on a true adventure.

"Now we can learn what it really means to take flight," she said. Once we were aboard Hook's ship, she released my hand and made her way toward the mast. Her grace and agility on the set made her look more like Tinkerbell than Wendy. This was a different Sylvia, one I hadn't even known existed until this moment. "Follow me and we can get lost long enough to forget." She smirked, a glimmer of mischief in her eyes.

"Forget what?"

"Forget that in here we're safe and that out there," she pointed toward the theatre doors. "Out there, we're nothing." She smiled, ascending the rope ladder up the mast. Once she reached the second level, she looked down at me, dangling her feet. "What, are you scared?"

I took the rope into my hands, followed up after her. A sensation pulsed through my body—first through my skin and then in my neck. It seized my heart. I thought it was love until I realized it was the pill. When I took my place next to Sylvia, we looked down on Neverland and London sharing the same stage. "I thought that I'd never get a chance with you."

"I thought love was bullshit," she laughed, loud and from her belly. "And then I go and meet you. You think that you're charming but you're not. I want to hate you."

"I don't believe you think love is bullshit," I said. "And you don't hate me. If you did, you wouldn't be sitting here with me right now."

"I'm sitting here because I have nowhere else to go." She turned toward the darkness, hiding her expression from me. I thought back to the guy in the car and his nasty cigar. I wouldn't have wanted to go back to that either.

"That guy in the car, was that your dad?"

She sniffled, then laughed. "No, not my dad."

"Uncle? Brother? Boyfriend?"

"It's complicated, Sam." It was the first time I'd heard her speak my name.

"Did he give you the pills?"

"I really don't want to talk about it." Her voice went hoarse as she dangled her feet over the cardboard ocean waves. I put my arm around her and she jerked away at first, but finally let me settle in. I trembled. It felt so good being that close to her.

"For what it's worth, I'm here for you, Sylvia." I felt like a walking cliché, but what else could I say to her? I refrained from reaching out to hold her hand or kiss her on the lips or embrace her tighter. I can still feel the enclosure of that silence. The high from those mysterious pills. The expanse of the theatre. That blurred line between reality and make-believe on that stage... It's the same thing I felt when I realized I was dead.

"Are you ready?" Sylvia asked.

"Ready for what?

"To fly," she said, taking my hand as she began her free fall from the mast. We plummeted toward the stage, fingers entwined. I envisioned us breaking our bones, shattering into pieces, scattering like fairy dust. But we never touched the ground. She led me up into the rafters, swooped around beams, and glided above the rows of empty seats. I still try to look back and understand the science behind all this, but the only thing that really matters is that for that one night, we flew.

ᏣᎳ

With opening night in a week, I started to get behind on my homework. I should have studied harder for my midterms, put some effort into the steel miniature windmill that counted for half of my Materials Processing grade, and not cheated on my trigonometry test by inputting answers into a secret file on my TI-83 graphic calculator. Instead of studying, I either rehearsed for the play or composed love poems for Sylvia. Otherwise I'd spend the nights tossing and turning, worrying about her, the pills, and the fact that even though we had flown hand in hand that night, we had not yet defined the terms of our relationship. I wanted Sylvia to see that I could be her real Peter Pan. I wanted to fend off her Captain Hook, the creep from the car. I wanted to love Sylvia freely. *Good form*—in the novel, Peter Pan didn't even know he had good form. Only Hook could see it, and he was nothing but jealous of Peter's ability to exist, fight, live, and love with no effort at all. After our night together in the empty theater, Sylvia didn't speak to me outside of rehearsal. She acted like us flying together never happened.

Opening night was a total disaster. Backstage, a little before the curtain would rise, I saw Mrs. Chabbock questioning Sylvia, the pink pill bottle in her hands. Someone must have found it on the pirate ship. Sylvia was crying, drops of mascara-tinted tears staining the top of her blue dress.

"They're not hers," I said, stepping forward. "They're mine."

"My heart is broken," Mrs. Chabbock said mournfully. Sylvia's eyes found mine. I prayed that she wouldn't contradict me in front of Mrs. Chabbock. "I can't let you do the play. I have to call your parents and tell them about this." She guided me to her office, sat me down, and said, "Where did you get the pills, Sam?"

"I found them," I said. All I could picture was Sylvia's face. Would she even care that I wasn't there to do the play?

"Such a shame," Mrs. Chabbock said. "Such a waste of talent." She filled out paperwork without speaking and then called my parents. I didn't care what consequence I would face if it meant that Sylvia wouldn't get in trouble.

⟨⟨∞∞⟩⟩

My parents took me home and lectured me. It was time to make some necessary life changes: commit to my schoolwork, pull my head out of the clouds. I stayed home from school the next day because I was facing expulsion. I spent the whole day online, staring at Sylvia's profile pictures. My sister Zoe came home, took one look at me, and said, "You need an intervention." We got in her car, drove to Tom's Famous Lemonade, and smoked cigarettes in the parking lot, an offer made only in case of an "existential crisis." I told her about the night that Sylvia and I flew.

"I would like you to know that I think this is all a load of shit," Zoe said. "None of this adds up, and now you're up a creek."

"I don't care about school. I don't care about the play. All I care about is Sylvia. I got the pills from her, and I have no idea where she got them from."

She passed me a fresh cigarette.

"I'm taking you to her," Zoe said. She started the car and barreled out of the lemonade stand parking lot. "The play should be letting out in ten minutes, right?"

"They banned me from the premises," I said.

"Maybe so," she said, "but they can't ban you from loving someone." Her cigarette dangled from her mouth as she drove. The breeze from the Maumee River blew in through her windows and carried ashes past my face. We sped down Bancroft Avenue, the empty warehouses and neon bar lights swirling past us in a blur. Zoe pulled up to TSA with a screeching stop. From outside the school, I heard applause and whistles. *Peter Pan* was a success—my understudy had kissed Sylvia, and the crowd had probably loved their chemistry. I bet nobody had even realized that I was gone.

"Go get her," Zoe said. I stepped out of the car and she peeled off down the street. I listened to the applause fade away and waited for Sylvia, knowing I'd see her hood-covered head trying to escape the area unseen. When the theatregoers exited the school, I spotted her patched hoodie moving briskly through the crowd, her eyes glued to the sidewalk.

"Sylvia!" I yelled. She didn't slow down, so I ran. When I caught up to her, I could see mascara running down her cheeks again. I took her by the hand and guided her across the street. Her hands were cold from the winter breeze drifting by way of the river. I put them to my face.

"I wasn't sure if I would see you," she said and pulled her hands away, burying them in her hoodie pouch.

"I got a misdemeanor and probation," I said. "It could have been a lot worse."

"I'm sorry you can't do the play," she said. Her eyes began to glisten in the glow of the street lamps.

"I only did the play for you," I said. A car pulled up beside us. It was the rusted Buick, its headlights gleaming in our eyes. The same guy sat at the wheel, a lit cigar clenched between his grinning teeth. I tried to keep her there with me, but she pulled away and got into the car without another word. My heart devolved into something less palpable than muscle, more tenacious than rock.

As the Buick rolled down the street I began to sprint. The guy behind the wheel didn't see me chasing until they came to a stop sign. I lunged forward, grappling the edge of their fender in my hands. He turned the corner and I hit the pavement, tumbled to the curb. As I fell, my gaze caught an image of him laughing and Sylvia's horrified face. I stood up and sped after them. I was afraid I would lose her forever. If I could fly, I'd be able to catch up to them. I needed the magic from the night that we had flown, but the pills had all been confiscated. In pursuit of Sylvia, I leapt over hydrants, puddles, and steel grates. Each time, I thought for certain my body would catch the wind just right and the Buick's taillights would once again be in arm's reach. No matter what, I wouldn't let Sylvia go back with that man. I imagined him taking her to some trailer park, smoking cigarettes while she cooked dinner. The streetlights above me flickered each time I passed beneath one. A domino effect of lights blinking out followed me en route to Sylvia, like stars on the road winding into an earthbound constellation on the way to Neverland. "Second star to the right, and straight on till morning!" The faster I went, the more indistinguishable the road became from the sky. Suddenly a singe of heat coursed through my body, the same feeling I had gotten from Sylvia's pills. Maybe the chemical was still in my system. I jumped into the air and didn't stop until I was side by side with her. She rolled down her window, her hair flailing in the riverside breeze.

"I won't let you go," I said. I held on to the Buick, one hand on the passenger side mirror, one on the door handle. My legs hovered, parallel to the vehicle. She unbuckled her seat belt, leaned her head out of the window, and kissed me. Suspended in air, our bodies developed their own gravitational pull. Flying above the Maumee River, we defied the logic of love, reinvented the laws of physics.

This is the last moment of my life I can review—my body soaring above the Maumee River, hand in hand with Sylvia. If I ever hit the water, I have no memory of it. The split second between life and death felt like when I auditioned for *Peter Pan*, stepping away from the curtain and into the character, soul detaching from body. Now I'm trapped here in death, watching myself meet Sylvia and leave her over, and over, and over again. Peter Pan never wanted to grow up, so he flew away to Neverland. I, on the other hand, never wanted to be out of love with Sylvia, and now, I never will be.

The Reincarnations

*A*my had gotten sick some weeks after her Nana died, and she was feeling bad because the grown-ups were sad all over again.

"I don't want to be sick anymore," Amy told her mother, the thermometer making it hard to speak. "I want to go outside and play butterfly."

She loved the wearable butterfly wings she'd gotten from Santa, maybe even more than her mermaid doll.

"I told you not to talk when we're taking your temperature," her mother said, "or we have to put the thermometer in your armpit."

Amy's eyes opened wide; she hated how cold the thermometer felt against her skin. She kept her lips sealed tight until she heard the thermometer beep. Her mother took it from her mouth and read the little numbers. *Oh no*, Amy thought, trying to gauge her mother's expression, *she's sad again.*

"Andie!" her mother called out. "Get the car ready. We need to take your sister to the ER."

"Okay, I'm on it," Andie called back. Amy loved her sissy; she was glad Andie was back home from California. Amy was still really little—almost too little to remember—when Andie moved away with Neal, and it broke her heart not being able to see her big sister for long periods of time. But it was a lot of fun when her mom and dad went to visit Andie and Neal because they went to Disneyland and got stuck in Neverland.

That was the most fun I ever had, Amy thought.

She'd loved Neal, too. He was like a big brother, but she wasn't allowed to talk about him or his silly jokes or how he tried to teach her to play the ukulele anymore. Not since he broke up with Andie and made her move back to Ohio. Amy was sad for her sissy, especially because she cried and cried forever. But Amy was happy, too, because Andie had come back home.

"Mommy, what's the ER?"

Her mother exhaled and said, "It's just the doctor, my love. You wait here in bed, okay? Mommy's going to pack some things and then we're going to leave."

"Can I take my mermaid?"

Her mother smiled and kissed her forehead.

"Of course, you can take your mermaid."

As soon as her mother left the room, Amy crawled out of bed and went over to the big aquarium by the window. When she'd found the caterpillar—Catty—in the yard, her dad helped her keep it safe. They put it in the aquarium with sticks and leaves and fed it bug food. Amy was shocked to find a cocoon formed soon after that; and now, the cocoon had been there for almost two weeks.

When she found Catty, she held it in her palm and thought about what Neal had once told her about reincarnation. They'd just buried her hamster—Twinkie—in the backyard, and nothing could console her except for Neal and his ukulele. She'd asked him where things go when they died, even though she already knew the answer: heaven. Or at least that's what everyone else had always told her. But Neal said, "I believe in reincarnation." She'd asked what reincarnation was—she'd always been good with big words, could even say the biggest one (supercalifragilisticexpialidocious)—and he said that it's when a soul goes somewhere else when something dies and is born as a new thing. "Like recycling," he'd said with a smile.

When she first held Catty in her palm, she'd wondered if it was the reincarnation of Nana. And now that Catty was in its cocoon, it was going to turn into a new thing all over again. Sometimes, especially right before she fell asleep, Amy wondered if she was a reincarnation. In her dreams, which she told nobody about, not even Andie, she dreamed she was so many different things. One time she was a giant snake that ate a man; one time she was a bird-woman who fell out of a lighthouse; once, an alligator; once, Tinker Bell.

"I thought I told you to stay in bed, little lady."

Amy spun around to find her mother standing in the doorway, holding the mermaid doll.

꧁꧂

Amy didn't want to go to the ER, even though her tummy felt like she was going to throw up and the world felt like it was blurry. Doctors and hospitals made her think of Nana, which made her think of death.

In the ER, Andie sat with Amy while their mother talked to the doctors. Amy leaned against Andie, who kept saying, "Don't worry, bummy, you're going to be okay."

"Why are you crying?" Amy asked.

Andie sniffled. "Because I love you more than anything in the world."

Amy felt so weak when the doctor put the stethoscope on her that she didn't jump, even though she hated cold things on her skin.

"Do I got ammonia?" Amy asked the doctor. She remembered her Nana talking about ammonia before she died.

"No, I'm afraid it's not pneumonia," the doctor said. He asked to talk to their mother in the hallway.

"Wait here," their mother said. "Your father should be here any minute."

Andie nodded, and Amy asked her for the mermaid doll.

She held the doll in her hands and thought about how nice it would be to live underwater like a mermaid. It would be so much cooler down there instead of how hot she felt now, so hot in her own skin.

"She's so pretty," Andie said. "Does she have a name?"

"Maybe I was a mermaid in my reincarnation," Amy said.

She looked up to Andie and saw tears streaming down her face.

"What do you mean, bummy? Where did you get that idea?"

Amy thought about Neal. "I'm not supposed to talk about it," she said.

Andie held her closer. "Maybe you were a mermaid."

"Maybe in my next reincarnation I'll be a caterpillar," Amy said. "Or maybe I'll be a butterfly."

Acknowledgements

*M*any thanks to Charlie, Brandon, and the rest of the team at Montag Press for making this collection a reality.

I'd also like to thank the editors at each literary journal where these stories first appeared.

My endless gratitude goes out to the writers and teachers who helped guide me: Alma Luz Villanueva, Alistair McCartney, Francesca Lia Block, Peter Selgin, Steve Heller, Gary Phillips, Jane Bradley, and Kyle Minor. And thank you to my early readers/workshop mates: Andrea Auten, Katy Avila, Stephen Desjarlais, Alex Thurner, and so many other great friends and writers from the Antioch University Los Angeles MFA program.

Thank you, Alexi, for your undying support and belief.

Thank you, reader, for lending your imagination to these stories.

Publication Credits

"The Alligator Theory" was a finalist in *The Saturday Evening Post* 2020 Great American Fiction Contest and first appeared in *Best Short Stories from The Saturday Evening Post Great American Fiction Contest 2020*.

"Property Damage" first appeared in *Eclectica Magazine*.

"The Al Capone Suite" first appeared in *The Blotter*.

"Andie Comes Home" first appeared in *Toledo City Paper*.

"Right Now at This Very Moment" first appeared in *Birdville Magazine*.

"The Naga Dreams" first appeared in *Red Fez*.

"Separation Anxiety" first appeared in *Philosophical Idiot*.

"Halcyon" first appeared in *Drunk Monkeys*.

"Family Business" first appeared in *Monzano Mountain Review*.

"Love Drugs" first appeared in *Barnstorm Journal*.

"Taking Flight" first appeared in *Fterota Logia*.

"The Reincarnations" first appeared in *Linden Avenue Literary Journal*.

About the Author

*N*athan **Elias** grew up in Toledo, Ohio. A former filmmaker, Nathan earned his MFA in Creative Writing from Antioch University Los Angeles. His short fiction, poetry, essays, and book reviews have appeared in publications such as *PANK*, *Entropy*, *Hobart*, *Pithead Chapel*, and *Barnstorm*, and he was a finalist of *The Saturday Evening Post* 2020 Great American Fiction Contest. He now lives in Nashville, Tennessee with his wife and rescue dog. *The Reincarnations* is his debut story collection.

Made in the USA
Columbia, SC
24 December 2020